CRACKS IN YESTERDAY

CRACKS IN YESTERDAY

ZELDA SPARK

Zelda Spark

For my mother and partner in crime...

"There is a crack in everything, that's how the light gets in."
Leonard Cohen

| 1 |

"Can you believe this weather?! I hardly had any customers today willing to drive through all this snow. I really hope this storm won't last too long or I'll have to close and wait for it to clear out. Oh, well, it's not like we don't know the drill. So, how are things going on your end?" Polly asked half concerned, half amused.

Taylor smiled back softly and shrugged his shoulders releasing a soft sigh.

"Things are ok. I guess you can't blame 'em for not coming out, it's a terrible drive in this weather. As a matter of fact, I'm off work starting this very moment, I've got the whole week off now that I've done nearly everyone's shift during the holidays. I'm just getting enough stuff to survive the week up there without starving to death," Taylor answered with a subtle grin.

"Oh how nice! Good for you, you deserve a break. I hope you get all the rest you need and come back to us all fresh and relaxed," Polly shot back with a huge smile that hid the rest of her face.

Polly was in her fifties and had not lost her looks. She was a pleasant, helpful and kind-hearted person. She opened her own store a little over a year ago, her husband Henry being the town's doctor and the only one for miles around, he had quite a lot of work. Polly needed distraction and felt the need to see more people so when old Mr. Winbote decided to sell his store she jumped on the occasion.

"Thanks, Polly, I will, trust me. Nothing beats being at home and watching the snow falling outside the windows."

Polly smiled back and walked to the counter as Taylor paid and went back to his car with a week's supply. He had been longing for this vacation more than the other years. He enjoyed taking the week off when everyone else was going back to work after the holidays. He had gotten used to it now. It used to be a hard time of the year for him to deal with before. It was still difficult but working hard kept his mind off things instead of speculating on what he had lost or what life could have been like if. IF.

Fate.

Fate had really taken its toll on Taylor's life. After losing both his parents and his young wife in a terrible car accident three years ago, he was left pretty much to his own self ever since. Yet, he never expressed his sorrow nor anger but his overall humor had changed. His bright blue eyes had lost their sparkle. He always remained extremely calm and was not one to talk much, only when necessary. He never got angry, sad nor even happy. One who would meet him would find him rather shallow and emotionless. Nothing could be read on his face, but the people of Blackmont knew him well and knew his story, and were very kind to him in a respectful way. No one ever mentioned the subject as if a page of history had been erased. Erased to keep him calm. After the accident, he had taken over his grandparents' ranch, up in the hills, and applied for the town police department as a patrol officer with the Sheriff's help. It kept his mind off things and made him feel useful despite the lack of serious trouble in town.

The night was starting to fall, even if the entire day had been quite dark with thick snow falling from the still heavy sky. Taylor had about an hour's drive to get home through the snow-covered roads. He did not mind driving even in such conditions. He was used to it, half of the year the road to his grandparents' ranch was covered with snow. The accident had not had that effect on him. Nothing did actually. He just went on as if nothing had happened.

As he fastened his seatbelt and was about to start the engine he made a quick list in his head of all the things he needed before leaving town. He did not want to have to drive back during his vacation.

"There's nothing I can't live without," he finally said to himself determined as he started the car and got out of Polly's Country Foods' parking lot with Johnny Cash singing through the speakers. He had only been driving ten minutes when the Sheriff called.

"I hope it's not a dinner invitation," he muttered to himself again as he hesitated to answer the phone.

"Hey, Sheriff."

"Hey Taylor, I just noticed that you were gone and that I didn't even wish you a good vacation. So take care and call if you need anything, sonny," said Sheriff Allister in a kind and paternal tone.

"Thanks, Sheriff, will do!" Taylor replied half-relieved, half-shameful, and hung up.

Neither of them was very talkative people. Sheriff Allister was the person who had had to break the bad news to Taylor three years ago. He had, since then, in some strange way, become a father figure for Taylor. He helped him enter the police department to keep him busy and have an eye on him. He was never too present but still there in case any help was needed. He watched over Taylor discretely and distantly. Taylor in exchange had great respect for Allister and never took advantage of their relationship.

Taylor looked at the green light and noticed he had been daydreaming again. It was now dark, he snapped out of it and started driving again. Sometimes his mind would run out like that but never when he was working. He was a very serious and hard-working person. He never complained about anything. Probably the employee any boss would dream of having.

A loud noise suddenly covered Johnny Cash's voice, Taylor looked around to see where it was coming from. Right in front of him, he saw an old pickup truck driving extremely fast from the top of the hill. The noise was creaky and Taylor had to cover his ears as it came closer and passed him by.

"That sucks, sounds like the transmission is broken, good luck getting it to the garage," he muttered to himself feeling sorry for the driver.

Taylor had never quite been the mechanical type. All he

wanted was a car that worked well and that he could trust. His father was a mechanic and would have wanted Taylor to take over the business but Taylor preferred spending time at his grandparents' ranch with the horses and the cattle. After the accident, he sold the garage to a school-friend for a good price. In exchange, he got his car repaired and serviced for free. Life was easy for Taylor. He had his routine, nothing very exciting or unexpected in a small town such as Blackmont, Montana. Nothing truly exciting apart from the scenery.

The landscape was not just plain beautiful but breathtaking. That's what had brought his grandparents there, that and the price of the land back then. It was good land considering the price, that's what his grandfather repeated all the time. No one really wanted to settle up there because of the snow, it snows a lot, not all year, there is what could be called a Summer. It just didn't last very long. Taylor always loved it there, he never felt the need to go anywhere else. Though he loved reading and watching movies he never felt the urge to go out and see things for himself. Even in his police work, there was nothing exciting going on, apart from a few old merry drunkards once in a while, not much to stir up the department. There weren't many people his age still living there. Most of them had set out as soon as they could to find jobs or just move to bigger cities. They would come back once in a while to visit their family, especially for the holidays. On rare occasions, young adventure-thirsty teenagers would come to snowboard on the untouched snowy hills which was dangerous considering there was no proper rescue team nor hospital for miles.

What Taylor had in mind as he was making his way through the snowy roads was lighting up the chimney as soon as he got home. He had collected just enough logs to last several weeks. He was looking forward to taking a nice warm bath with a cup of fresh-brewed French Roast coffee. And then, he couldn't decide what he was more in the mood for, reading a book or watching a DVD? Just thinking of his evening's program, he felt all relaxed and surprised himself with a silly lingering smile on his face when something pulled him out of that comfortable feeling. Something caught his eyes. He strained his eyes to make out what it was through the icy mist. After a few seconds, he could make out head-lights, not coming in his direction, but perfectly still facing the other way. He slowed down to take a better look as he approached the lights. At first, he thought the car was parked there and waiting but as his eyes adapted to the darkness he could see the car had crashed into two gigantic trees.

For a moment, his heart had stopped beating, and he had trouble breathing. When his spirits finally came back to him he reached out for the flashlight he kept in the glove compartment and stepped out of the car. The snow was already deep and thick. He painstakingly walked towards the other car and pointed the flashlight through the driver's window and saw what seemed to be a woman's head against the stir-ring-wheel. He tried to open the door but it was locked. It was freezing cold and the snow was starting to frost the car.

Without hesitation, he broke the car window with the other end of his flashlight. He unlocked the door and after tugging at it quite hard it finally opened. He slightly lost balance and almost fell backward as it opened. He managed to unfasten the driver's seatbelt and took a look around the car to see if there were any other passengers. Seeing she was alone he started getting her out of the car. She seemed unconscious. He carried her to his car and laid her delicately in the trunk. He wanted to call for help but it was no use, up there he was out of range. He had to head back home to make that call from his landline. As he got back behind the wheel he analyzed the road one last time trying to figure out what could have happened.

From the marks on the road, it seemed as though a car coming from the opposite direction forced this car off the road and into those trees. Taylor knew this road well and couldn't help but think that if it weren't for those trees the car would have fallen into the ravine. As he arrived and drove into the driveway he suddenly remembered that old noisy pickup that passed him by earlier on. He carried the girl from his trunk to the living room. He settled her as carefully as he could on the big old leather couch. Her head was bleeding. His shaky fingers dialed Allister's number.

"Tim?"

"Taylor? What's wrong?" Allister asked confused. Taylor never called him Tim.

"An accident, not me, a car, on my way home, up in the hills, a girl, her head is bleeding. I don't know what to do. I brought her to my place. Maybe I should bring her back to town to Henry's clinic?"

"Keep calm, does she have a pulse?"

"Pulse, right, hold on." He hated himself for not having thought of that on his own. He rushed to check.

"Yeah, her heart's beating, it's faint but it's beating."

"Okay, let me call Henry, and we'll be right there, no use driving her to the clinic Henry isn't there anymore, since he had no patients he went home with Polly to wait for the storm to end. In the meantime, put a wet towel on her forehead and a pillow under her neck. Check if she's growing a fever."

"What? You're going to drive all the way up here with Henry right now? It's not a good idea Sheriff. Let's wait till tomorrow."

"It'll be okay sonny, don't forget I'm used to it! We'll be there soon."

After doing what Allister had told him to do, he set up a fire. So much for his evening plans. For the first time in a long while, Taylor was feeling upset. The calmness that had inhabited him since the accident had been disturbed. He felt uneasy and useless regarding this girl lying unconscious in his home. He waited for what seemed ages before Allister and Henry arrived.

As Henry examined the girl, Allister and Taylor drove back to her car to investigate. They both took some notes and Allister took some photos of the scene. When they were finished they collected all the things that were in the car and brought them back to Taylor's. In all, there was a handbag, a suitcase, and a guitar. Allister agreed with Taylor regarding what had happened. The girl was obviously avoiding a car speeding down her way when she crashed into the trees.

"She's lucky as hell if you ask me. If it weren't for those trees, she would be dead." Allister realized too late after the words had slipped his mouth, that those words in Taylor's ears couldn't have had a neutral reception. He put his hand on Taylor's shoulder silently, the look they exchanged was as heavy in meaning as any words could express. They headed back to the house.

"She's fine, nothing broken. She'll probably wake up with a headache or neck pain. I gave her a shot of painkillers to calm the pain and here are some pills for later. The best is she doesn't move, at least not before a couple of days," said Henry.

Taylor nodded and shook both men's hands and told them to be careful on their way home.

Taylor stood in front of the empty bed, in the bedroom he hadn't been in for years. He changed the sheets, dusted the room, and set up a fire. He carried twenty-five-year-old Estelle into the freshly made bed. He put all her things, except her purse, in a corner of the room. He hesitantly left her there to pursue his evening plans.

He headed back to his car to get the groceries and hoped he would have enough supplies as he now had a surprise guest to feed as she would eventually wake up. So many things were going through his mind as he was stocking up the fridge and cupboards. He did everything mechanically and without focus. His face and his whole body were tense. So tense that he had to stretch his spine and neck without being able to relax. The vision of his long-awaited and desired bath popped back into his head and after a little hesitation, he finally decided to go ahead and succumb to his plans.

He quickly checked up on the girl before heading to his room. The thought and preparation momentarily turned his thoughts away from the situation but as he lay soaking up in the bathtub with a hot cup of coffee he somehow could not relax. His thoughts kept wandering off to the stranger that was sleeping in his grandparent's bed. Gradually his thoughts turned into an urge of curiosity. He wanted to go through her purse to find out who she was. He tried to resist the temptation of going through her personal belongings but after internally debating whether he should or should not he ended up convincing himself that after all, it was part of his job to do so. After all, he was a police officer. He couldn't be judged for simply doing his job. Yet he still tried to relax but nothing worked.

He grew more and more restless in that bathtub that had become more and more uncomfortable with his body temperature peeking up and the sweat pouring down his face he could not take another second and opened the tap to pour a certain amount of cold water. As his body temperature lowered to normal he finished his coffee in one gulp and got out of the tub, grabbed a towel, and ran to his room to put his pajamas on. He headed to the living-room table where the purse had been left by Allister, who had looked through it to find her ID. He tried hard to focus on something else to do. He did have a whole pile of DVDs he had ordered and hadn't found time to watch. He went through them to see what kind of movie he was in the mood for but only one thing obsessed him, the purse. The damn purse. Why? Why couldn't he just be his usual self, uninterested? Why this sudden burst of curiosity?

"Damn it," he whispered to himself nervously scratching his unshaven chin. He hadn't shaved in three days and it was starting to itch. He made it a rule never to shave when he was on vacation. At that precise moment, it seemed that his long-awaited vacation was somewhat ruined. He couldn't help but feel angry. Angry against that poor girl who crashed into the trees, or was he angry against the crazy old pickup, or was it something else? His plans were ruined, and Taylor wasn't used to that. Nothing would come unexpected enough to ruin his plans. Before he even realized it, his hands had already gotten a hold of the shiny red purse. The purse was huge and heavy.

"What the hell does she carry around in this?"

He started dissecting the insides: a wallet, a black varnished one with illustrated tattoo designs on it. Fifty-seven dollars and tons of coins, tons of credit cards, and store receipts. No pictures. A French driver's license and passport along with a work VISA. A bunch of cards, a whole pack of some band's stickers, and several copies of that band's album. An agenda. He put the agenda aside saving it for later as he continued inventorying the contents of the purse. Perfume, Chanel number 5, red lipstick, still Chanel, more make-up, black nail polish and at the bottom of the purse several pink guitar picks, three little black notebooks and pens, chewing gum, Altoids, tissues, anti-bacterial gel, Advil, more coins and empty wrappers. He put the notebooks aside along with the agenda. Last but not least in the side pocket a BlackBerry. He also put it aside.

Having quenched his thirst for curiosity he felt quite satisfied with his discoveries and the lingering excitement of the further analysis of the items he had collected. Taylor put everything but the agenda, notebooks, and BlackBerry, back inside the purse. He eagerly took the agenda and started going through it page by page. The beginning of the year had nothing written on it except birthdays. Around mid-April, things were written here and there, some in French, others in English. Mostly flight and hotel information as well as appointments. She apparently spent a week in Seattle in May and was busy meeting a certain Dan from A & R almost every day. Later on, in September she came back to Seattle but this time with no return date mentioned. She had a weekly appointment with Dan on Wednesdays. Mid-October there were three days marked studio and that's it. Nothing more.

Taylor wasn't as satisfied as he'd expected to be by the content of the agenda. As he put the agenda down he picked one of the three black notebooks up. They were all three miscellaneously filled with unfinished stories, lists of words scribbled some rhyming others not. He read each word as if they would unlock a key to some kind of mystery. He was intrigued. He paused and thought about it for a while, his mind drifting off. When he snapped back into it he decided to take a look at her BlackBerry, which had no network. Her incoming calls were almost all from that same Dan. Taylor jumped to his senses and decided not to go through her text messages and emails, which he judged to be way too private and unjustifiable. He put everything back into the purse and brought it into the bedroom with the rest of her belongings.

He checked her forehead for a temperature again and she seemed fine. She was breathing deeply and her face looked peaceful lying there, her long wavy ginger hair upon the white pillow. Her make-up was all smudged, yet she seemed awkwardly attractive despite that. He realized that he had left her on the bed in her boots and jeans. Judging it was not comfortable for a good rest he rummaged through her suitcase in search of something for the night. After carefully taking her boots and jeans off he managed to delicately remove her sweater managed to slip her into the closest thing to a nightgown he could find. As he did so he discovered a detailed tattoo spreading from her neck to her shoulder. He could only make out a phoenix, which seemed entwined with a gypsy face. He put her under the covers and tried to wash her face the best he could with a warm wet towel before placing a glass of water on the nightstand in case she woke up during the night. All this done he decided to go to bed as well.

That night was as quiet as ever. The silence, which normally never bothered him, kept him from falling asleep. Every single breeze or crack in the house startled him and made his heart pace. He breathed in deeply and out slowly to calm down and relax. Several hours of struggle later, sleep had finally crept into him when the sound of shattering glass violently broke it again. He raced to his grandparents' room but the glass of water was exactly where he had left it and the girl was sound asleep. Confused, he walked back to his room and fell asleep without any trouble this time but the ringing of the phone tore him from his sleep once more. When he gradually realized it was really ringing he grabbed the phone.

"Taylor speaking."

"Hi Taylor, it's Tim. How's everything going? Has she woken up yet?"

"Hey, no, not yet. I put her to bed, and she hasn't moved an inch since. Got anything new about her or the other car?"

"I ran her plates, it's a rental, she just switched from a Mustang to a Landrover, told the rental place she was going on a road trip and needed a car she would feel safe in. The rental place is going to send up an expert as soon as the snow stops.”

“Did you tell them that it was obviously not her fault?”

“Yeah, I told them but I’m sure it won’t make a difference, depends on the waiver she got. By the way, I know it’s messing up your vacation so don’t worry about it, I’ll make sure it’s extended.”

“Thanks, we’ll see about that later,” Taylor said half-focused.

“Well, call me when she wakes up and I’ll give you a call if I get more info.”

“Ok, boss.”

Taylor hung up and stared at the door blankly, it was still snowing heavily outside meaning he would need to start clearing out the snow from his front door. He couldn’t even process the thought of getting out of bed. The feeling of comfort and warmth intensified as the thought of having to cope with the cold outside crept upon him. Before he knew it his mind was already off listing all the different things he had to get done. He narrowed them down to two major ones: feeding and brushing Shakespeare and then shoveling away the snow from the front door.

There was a heavy stillness in the air that pinched Taylor’s inner turmoil. One he had never been accustomed to. It wasn’t the past that slapped him in the face but the future. He felt things would never be the same, he knew something inside him had changed and it frightened him. He didn’t know if he had to fear this newcomer or welcome it like a savior.

Not that he was a believer. Before the accident, he would occasionally go to church for his parents, but he never stepped into one since the funeral. He never whispered a prayer either. He felt fate wasn't the work of God because if it had been, he wouldn't have lost all the ones he loved.

Questions were subject to pain, so he evinced them until they never even showed up again. Each day rose and faded with bare necessities like going to work, eating, driving, sleeping, and with things such as the weather, the seasons, familiar faces, familiar places. No questions asked from outside nor inside. Plainly inhabiting a body. In this case a strong and young man's body.

Taylor was a somewhat rugged but handsome man even though he never paid attention to his appearance. He didn't care. He was an only child and was very close to his grandmother until she passed away when he was sixteen. She loved Shakespeare, and she would read him plays every time he came to the ranch. She had been an actress before meeting his grandfather and had kept that little *folie* very alive. Her parents had immigrated to Virginia from England. She had left her family very young to join a traveling theater company. She never saw her family again. By the time the company reached Salt Lake City, she was twenty-one. That is where she met Taylor's grandfather, who at the time was working at the Trading Post. They met while he was repairing the company's car. She was tired of traveling around and had decided to stop and settle in Salt Lake City.

She found a job as a waitress since having an excellent memory and all that. But life there was expensive. One day they met a man who had just traveled to Canada and on his way back home he stopped in a town called Blackmont in Montana. He kept saying he'd sell everything he had and move there because it was the most beautiful place he'd ever seen.

The young couple talked it over for weeks when they finally decided to give it a try. It took them a while to get to Blackmont having to stop and work to pay their way up there. But as soon as they arrived the beauty of the place captivated them, just like the man had described it. In the beginning, they rented a room in the town restaurant, and Taylor's grandfather soon thought it was a good idea to build a garage. There was no mechanic in town, people had to go miles out to get to one. The people of the town helped him build the garage. When the garage was finally built, they lived on site. Over the years, people came to the town to start from scratch. Everybody was hardworking and thankful for what they had.

As Taylor's grandparents grew old they moved into the ranch they had been building up in the hills. They moved there and left their house next to the garage to their son. They had had their son quite late, their only child, he took over the garage at an early age. Fixing things had always fascinated him. He liked his job. His mother had tried to interest him in literature, but he preferred helping his father. Once up in the hills, they ran a nice little ranch with horses and cattle and as a child, Taylor spent a lot of time there. His parents were too busy running the garage. His grandmother did most of his schooling. That was until it got too difficult for her to help him. She had built up a huge library in the house and Taylor still added a considerable amount of books to it. He never watched television and was probably the only person in town without the internet.

As he entered the stable and approached Shakespeare, his horse, it occurred to him he wouldn't be able to go out for a ride as long as the girl was asleep. Even now, how would she react if she woke up in a room she had never seen before? He wondered if she would remember the accident or if, like many movies he'd seen, she'd be amnesiac. At the thought of all this, he did as fast as he could brushing and feeding Shakespeare, cleaning up his stall, and going back to check on her. The girl was still asleep but wasn't in the same position. He wondered if the shot Henry had given her would still affect her when she woke up. How was he going to deal with this? What if she didn't trust him? After all, why should she trust a perfect stranger after waking up in an empty house in the middle of nowhere? He should leave his police jacket in plain sight to help her feel safe. He hadn't thought about what her reactions could be to the situation until right that moment. So many things could come to her mind.

Work still had to be done so he started shoveling the snow, it took him nearly two hours as he interrupted every now and then to listen and check up on the girl. Now there were two huge piles of snow on each side. The child in him wanted to make snowmen out of them, but he resisted the urge. The phone started ringing inside and Taylor ran to pick up the receiver.

"Hi Taylor, it's Henry, just wanted to check if the girl had woken up yet?"

"Hey Henry, no she hasn't."

"Well, wait a little longer, but you'll have to try and wake her up before tonight, she needs to drink water and if possible eat something."

"Okay, I'll do my best and call you if there's a problem."

Taylor turned to the clock and saw it was already three in the afternoon. He scratched his head and tried to gather enough courage to do what he had been told to do. He didn't know what scared him most, not being alone anymore or her reaction, or perhaps that she didn't wake up.

| 2 |

"Sorry, I can't get to the phone right now, just leave a message and I'll call you back," went Estelle's voice on her voicemail for the tenth time.

"She's not answering! Why the hell isn't she answering her damn phone? This is why I hate working with women!" Dan grumbled annoyed.

"The landlord said she left the apartment three days ago. She gave her keys back and took all her things," replied his secretary.

"Spencer's gonna be real pissed off when he hears about this. I have a meeting but keep trying to get a hold of her."

Dan was boiling mad. They had had a serious fight the other night, the night before she left. They had been working a lot lately, seeing each other all the time, and he couldn't help but fall for her. He tried not to but after his divorce and everything, with his job addiction, he hadn't met anyone since. She didn't seem to mind all his little intentions, and he thought she appreciated them. But that night, it all went wrong. He had invited her to a nice restaurant, just the two of them, to celebrate all the good work they had achieved. Dan had signed Estelle onto the record label a few months ago and things were already starting to shape up. He had even made her leave France and come all the way to Seattle.

A lot of the work had started before she moved but things got to a point where she needed to be near. He knew it wasn't an easy thing for her, leaving all her friends and family behind and being all alone in a city she didn't know, but it didn't seem to bother her that much. He was the only person she really knew. Work keeping her busy and all. Well, Dan had grown very fond of her and thought it was mutual. She'd been going through a good deal and when Dan made it clear to her that night, his feelings for her, she jumped into a fury. Dan was light years away from expecting such a reaction and was hurt. Hurt both intimately but also professionally. It wasn't going to be easy to deal with, and he couldn't just tell someone to take over the project. In a few seconds, it felt like his world was crumbling down.

"That's why you made me come over here?! I can't believe it! I thought you were interested in my music," she said half yelling, half crying.

"Estelle, please, it's not what you think. Stop it with the clichés! Can't you just understand that I appreciate you and care for you and that all I did was because of that and not just because I wanted to get you into my bed? Is that too hard to understand? You of all people! Estelle, we've got to get through this misunderstanding, one way or the other. Let's not blow this, it's important, there's a contract, there's a deal. I'll let you calm down and think things over and I'll call you back in a day or two, once you've come to your senses," he managed to say quite calmly even though he was sinking through the wooden panels beneath his feet. Dan was known and respected for being professional. Sometimes he wanted to explode and let it all out. Yet he didn't.

Estelle remained silent, arms crossed and head down, as Dan walked out the door. He waited outside her door for a while, wishing she would come back to her senses and excuse herself, but she never came.

Dan's phone was vibrating; it was his secretary.

"Excuse me, I have to take this," he interrupted the meeting to answer.

"Sir, Estelle's parents just called the office. They're worried, they haven't heard from her in over a week. I don't know what to tell them. Should we tell them the truth or wait?"

Dan didn't feel the phone slipping out of his hand, he hadn't told anyone what had happened between Estelle and him. He was responsible for Estelle here in Seattle and was worried. He didn't have a clue where she could have gone.

"No use worrying them for now. Tell them she took some days off in the country and that's probably why they haven't heard from her."

Dan tried to remain focused till the end of the meeting, but he kept wondering where she had gone and if she were safe. But overall if she would ever come back. He wouldn't forgive himself if something had happened to her.

He knew she was happy to be here and to have finally signed to a record company. She had been trying to find a record deal for years in Paris but with no luck. She got tired of trying and was on the verge of letting everything down when Dan had contacted her. She didn't trust him at first, and he couldn't blame her, she had been let down so many times that believing people in the business had become difficult but there she was in Seattle now, the company had gotten her an artist VISA, an apartment, and a car.

They were working on promoting her debut album and Dan should never have expressed his feelings for her, not now, there was too much going on, too much they had to deal with still.

"I've really screwed things up this time," he muttered to his reflection in the mirror. He hit the wall with his fist so hard he couldn't even feel the pain. It was past midnight, and he was desperately waiting for his phone to ring.

| 3 |

The wind stuck the snow to the windows. The fireplace was blazing and the house felt comfortable and warm with the flickering reflections of the dancing fire on the walls. The only thing that interrupted the stillness of the place was the crackling of the burning logs and the wind embracing the house. Night had fallen and Taylor was busy in the kitchen. He wasn't much of a cook but managed pretty well with simple things. He was cooking chicken and mashed potatoes. The last thing he wanted to serve her was frozen pizza when she would wake up. A nice homemade supper was a lot more welcoming and it had been a while since he had cooked something. It was back when he had invited the Sheriff and his wife to thank them for inviting him nearly every week. Mrs. Allister was the nicest woman he knew. She could not have children, so they both considered Taylor like their own son. They were good friends with his parents, they had gone to school together and seen Taylor grow up.

"Who are you?" a fragile voice said breaking through the cloud of his inner thoughts.

Taylor looked up and there she was, standing in the kitchen doorway. Her right hand rubbing the back of her neck as if it could magically take the pain away. She seemed drowsy and weak.

"Oh, you're awake, are you feeling okay?" he managed to say in a comforting voice as he stopped what he was doing and put the wooden spoon down beside the pot.

She looked at him confused.

"Sorry, I'm Taylor, I'm a police officer here in Blackmont. I'm the one who found you. You were in a car accident last night. I brought you here, I live here. The roads are filled with snow but the Sheriff and the county doctor came up to check if you were okay last night. The doctor said you were fine. Are you feeling okay?" he was surprised the words kept pouring right out of his mouth without him controlling any syllable as he wiped his hands on the kitchen towel and walked towards her.

"An accident?" she said blankly still rubbing the back of her neck.

"Yes, about four miles away, you hit some trees. It looks as though something made you leave the road quite violently. Do you remember anything?"

She kept pushing her hand to her neck and head, she seemed in pain, and she shook her head.

He walked up to her and reached for the pills Henry had left.

"Is your head still aching a lot? The doctor said you would be in a little pain, and he left these pills for you to take if you felt any pain. They're painkillers. You should take some but first, you really have to eat something." His tone was calm and comforting.

Estelle felt puzzled but not insecure. He led her to a chair and sat her down gently. He served a plate of chicken and mashed potatoes for each of them. At first, she didn't seem inclined to eat but by the third mouthful her appetite grew and by the time Taylor had eaten half of his plate she had devoured all of hers.

"Well, glad to see you haven't lost your appetite," he said amused and handed her two pills and a tall glass of water.

She seemed to trust him, unlike what he had imagined.

"You want anything else?"

She looked at him thinking and shyly asked if he had any coffee.

"Sure thing, I'll make some right away." She lifted her hand to stop him.

"No, finish eating first, I can wait."

"I like having coffee with my meal, I'll make some now."

The kitchen smelled good and felt warm and cozy, cozier than it had felt in ages. The heat flowing out of the stove and the vapors of the brewing coffee made Estelle feel at home. For the first time since she had left France, she felt at home.

"Here you are," he said as he put a big cup of steaming coffee right in front of her with a smile.

"Thank you," she said with a faint childish voice as she took the cup and embraced it in both hands, brought it to her nose and took in a deep breath with her eyes closed, and inhaled the fragrance. At her first sip, she curled her shoulders with satisfaction.

"Is it that good?" Taylor asked teasingly.

She smiled and shut her eyes in confirmation. They both sat there, at the kitchen table, silent and comfortable, for a while.

"Let's move to the living room," he finally said breaking the silence.

He refilled both cups with coffee, and they moved to the living room. She stood in front of the fireplace to warm her hands and stared into the fire. He sat down on the sofa and watched her. She was not very tall, quite a petite figure but very elegant. When she noticed she was being observed she sat down holding the cup tightly in her hands and shivered.

"Are you cold? Do you want something warm to wear?" Taylor asked concerned.

"I'm okay, just a shiver from standing too long next to the fire. It's a nice place you've got here," she said looking around the room, the fire sparkling in her eyes. "So you were saying that my car hit some trees?"

Taylor thought she would never ask, he figured she didn't want to talk about it, so he didn't force her to.

"Yes, I was driving home when I saw your headlights, it's only when I pulled up and came close enough that I saw the car had crashed into the trees," he said gravely, the smile disappearing from his face.

She looked down as if she were trying to remember what had happened, and she started touching her neck again.

"Do you remember anything at all?" he asked in a low voice but there was no answer to his question.

She kept staring at the blazing fire and rubbing her neck. Before he knew it he was sitting beside her, his hand on her back.

"It's okay, it's common not to remember things in such circumstances. It might come back to you later. Maybe you should have some rest."

He helped her to the bedroom. She lay down and fell asleep almost instantly. It must have been the medicine kicking in. He stood there looking at her to make sure she was sleeping peacefully and went back to the living room.

He poured himself another cup of coffee and sat down in front of the fire. All of a sudden he realized he hadn't called Allister nor Henry back. He dialed Allister's number and told him the girl had woken up a little groggy but seemed to be doing fine. He explained she did not remember much for the moment but that she had a good appetite. Allister said he would let Henry know. They wished each other a goodnight and hung up. Taylor sat there in front of the fire lost in his thoughts for so long that his coffee had run cold. He didn't know what to do, he wasn't in the mood for a movie and obviously couldn't concentrate on a book, but he didn't feel sleepy.

He put more logs into the fire and turned the television on to watch the news. They were still announcing a lot of snow with an average of twenty degrees. Taylor fell asleep in front of the television. The wind was howling outside.

A frozen breeze woke Taylor up, he looked around to see the front door was wide open. He jumped up and paced to the door and saw nothing except for the white trees dancing in the moonlight. The beauty of the scene struck him. He closed the door unwillingly but the cold was unbearable. He walked over to Estelle's bedroom and saw the bed was empty. His heart started to race. He looked for her everywhere in the house but in vain. It was three in the morning. He grabbed his coat and headed outside. His car was still there and this time he saw footprints in the snow. It led to the stables. He ran to the stable and found Estelle asleep in a pile of hay. He carried her back to the house, she was freezing cold. She had walked bare-footed in the snow. He ran a hot bath and tried to wake her up. She opened her eyes and looked at him.

"What were you doing outside, are you crazy?" he said trying to control his anger.

She didn't seem to understand what he was talking about.

"What do you mean outside?" I didn't go anywhere.

He looked at her confused.

"I just found you asleep outside in the stables, you're frozen, and we have to get you warm again. The bath is ready, go ahead and take it. I'll get you something warm to drink."

He left her in the bathroom and went to the kitchen to make more coffee.

On his way to the kitchen, he double-locked the door for the first time. It wasn't a habit of his out here. He paused and stared at the melted drops of snow on the wooden floor. He took his sleeve and wiped them to avoid water stains. As he got back up his back cracked, and he cussed in his beard as he continued his way to the kitchen.

"I'm sorry," interrupted a shy voice.

"I'm really confused about all this. I don't remember going outside. Really I don't. The only explanation would be sleepwalking, but I don't sleepwalk, at least I haven't till now if that's the case," Estelle said standing in the doorway, a towel around her and water dripping down her hair.

"It's alright, I was just worried, you scared me. Well, maybe it's a consequence of the accident. I'll talk to the doctor about it. Till then, I'll just double lock all the doors," he said amused so that she could relax as he handed her a cup of coffee. She thanked him and took the cup.

"You don't happen to have whiskey by any chance?" she asked with a soft voice.

He looked at her surprised and said he did. He got out the bottle of Jack Daniels from the bar.

"It's bourbon, will that do?" he asked showing the bottle.

"Perfect." Handing him her cup, so he could add some to her coffee.

He did the same, and they both silently sipped away looking at each other from time to time.

"This is really awkward, I mean this whole situation," Estelle said.

"Where were you going? I mean what brought you around here? No one ever comes around here without a purpose."

"Well, I wish I could tell you." She looked down uneasily.

"You mean you don't remember anything at all?"

She shook her head and tears started running down her cheek, but she wiped them away as soon as she felt them.

Taylor looked at her blankly not knowing what to say.

"I remember being angry and leaving with all my things, but I don't know where I was going and I don't remember what happened. A complete blackout."

"Isn't there anyone you could call that would know what your plans were?"

"Not really," she said coldly.

She didn't want to call Dan. If someone knew anything it would be him. She vaguely remembered their fight. She felt cheated and betrayed. She didn't trust Dan anymore. She swallowed all that was left in her cup in one huge gulp. She forgot this perfect stranger was observing her every move. A stranger who felt surprisingly familiar. She never felt comfortable with people she had just met, so why this exception? What was so special about him, was it his composure? He poured her some more Jack Daniel's. She thanked him and drank it slowly this time.

"I should get some sleep," she said as she swallowed the last sip, her eyes shining from the alcohol, medicine, and exhaustion.

"Same for me," Taylor said getting up and helping her off the couch.

What was left of the night marched away as both were fast asleep. Nothing moved except for the hands of the clock. Taylor opened his eyes and saw it was eleven. He wasn't used to oversleeping. He got out of bed and headed to the kitchen to make breakfast. He found Estelle sitting in the kitchen, breakfast served on the table with a radiant smile. Taylor scratched his head in surprise.

"I hope you don't mind that I prepared breakfast?" she said noticing the look on his face. "I woke up early," she added.

"No, not at all, it's great, thank you. I'm just not used to waking up and having my breakfast ready," he answered still surprised as he sat down looking at what she had prepared.

"Oh, for a moment there I thought you were angry," she sighed in relief. "Hope you like scrambled eggs and bacon for breakfast, that's all I found in the fridge?"

"My favorite, it's perfect. Really."

She sat there smiling and sipping hot coffee.

"Last night you said you found me asleep in the stable. Does that mean you have a horse?" she asked curiously.

"Positive, you ride?"

"Not really, I just like horses, well animals, in general, to be more precise."

"You want to see him?"

"I'd love to!" she said jumping up.

She was radiant. Her eyes were bright and shiny. A ray of sunlight had managed to melt away a spot of snow and pierce through the white window right onto her eyes. Taylor chuckled, finished his plate and his coffee, and got up. He handed her a warm coat to walk to the stable. The stable was just as Taylor's grandfather had left it.

"It's beautiful," she said as her eyes were trying to take in as much information as they could.

Taylor smiled proudly and showed her the way to his horse.

"My grandfather built this place, it was his dearest dream."

Estelle approached the horse as slowly as possible not to

frighten him. She turned to Taylor and asked permission to pet him. Needless to say, permission was granted.

"It's alright Shakespeare, she's a friend."

"Shakespeare? How did you come up with a name like that for a horse?"

Taylor grinned and shrugged his shoulders.

"My grandmother, she loved Shakespeare and would read his plays to me all the time."

"That's sweet."

"You want to ride him?"

"Is it that obvious?" she replied all excited.

"Promise, as soon as the snow stops and that you feel better, you'll go out for a ride."

Estelle's look wandered off, transfixed in a stare with sadness settling upon her face.

"Do you mind brushing him while I clean the stable up then we'll see about fixing something for lunch, okay?" Taylor said to take her mind off whatever it was that made her drift away like that.

Once finished they headed back to the house. The minute they entered she took a deep breath of relief and sighed as if all of it could disappear in an instant as if it were a dream she did not want to awake from. Taylor was already busy in the kitchen when she walked in.

"How can I help?"

"No, you already took care of breakfast, lunch is on me!"

They had finished their meal and were having coffee when Estelle suddenly remembered something. He could tell something was going on by the look on her face.

"Is everything okay?" he asked worried.

"What day are we?" she asked as if she had missed something important.

"Sunday, why?"

"No, nothing, I just realized I didn't know what day we were. So the accident was Friday, right?"

"Exactly," he said waiting for her to say something else, maybe something she'd remembered, but nothing came.

She just sat there playing with the cup she had in her hands.

"I have some things to do around the house if you want to get some rest," he told her as he headed outside to shovel some snow again.

"Sure, no problem," she said.

| 4 |

Estelle went back to what she now considered her room. She grabbed her purse and went to bed. She lay flat on her stomach with her legs in the air and started taking everything out of her bag, just like Taylor had done the night of the accident. She reached for her Blackberry and searched for a specific email she had received. It was Dan informing her of an important meeting with a radio station programmer. It was on Tuesday. She knew how disappointed Dan would be if she didn't show up for that meeting. He had worked so hard to get that meeting.

Being a recognized singer-songwriter had always been her dream. Nothing else had been more important. As a consequence, she had very few friends, and she hardly ever saw her family. And now that wish seemed far away, almost lost and unreal. She had had her moments, moments of discouragement, when she wanted to give up on everything. Those moments hurt and were filled with anger and sadness. But not this time. She felt nothing. As if she weren't the same person anymore. She looked at her guitar and didn't even want to open the case.

She didn't know what she was going to do. Would she call Dan and tell him to forget about everything and really lose her one and only chance to do something or would she be able to deal with it all and try? Could she ignore all of it and work with Dan as if nothing had ever happened? She wasn't sure she'd have the strength. One thing was certain, she couldn't just stay there in the middle of nowhere and not tell anyone where she was. She couldn't even stay in the US if she didn't fulfill the contract she had with Dan. But she did not want to end this. She had never felt so free, paradoxically. Was this what freedom really was? No strings attached, unknown, invisible in the middle of nowhere?

She was miles from thinking that people could be worried by her silence because she did not care if they were. She didn't think of her parents. She called them once a week when she thought of it, but they had always been more interested in her career than in her. It hurt her to admit it but it was the truth. Her friends in Paris were all superficial, there was no one she could really count on and call when she was feeling low. No one she could call up in the middle of the night for no particular reason and just talk about her day. After all, what good is it living in a big city when all you really are is alone amidst millions of strangers? She was in the middle of nowhere with a person she did not even know, and she felt secure.

She stared at her reflection in the pocket mirror and saw a bruise on her left cheek which must've been from hitting the stirring-wheel. It was turning yellowish-orange. She realized she hadn't even taken a look at herself since. She decided to take a bath and fix herself up a little. She grabbed clean clothes from her suitcase and entered the blue-tiled bathroom.

The warm water felt so relaxing, she hadn't noticed how stressed she had been. She lay her head back and closed her eyes to appreciate every inch of her body within the water and the smell of the lavender soap.

As she did so she must have fallen asleep, at least for a while. She woke up startled by something, she thought Taylor had come in but there was no one there, the door was closed and the bathroom was empty except for her. Still, she felt she wasn't alone. She didn't feel insecure or anything. She closed her eyes again and before she knew it she had fallen asleep. In her sleep, she was in the bathtub, and in the corner, sitting in a chair was a woman, not young nor old, ageless, looking at her with a peaceful look on her face. She didn't recognize her, she had never seen that face before. She wanted to talk to her but no words could come out of her mouth when a firm grip pulled her forward and started shaking her...

"Estelle! Estelle!" Taylor was yelling as he shook her and lifted her from the water.

Estelle opened her eyes and gasped bewildered coughing out all the water she had swallowed.

"You could have drowned, you were drowning, didn't you feel it?" Taylor said upset and still a bit shaky.

"I wasn't sleeping," Estelle coughed out.

"Really, that's why it took you so much time to open your eyes after I took your head out of the water? You were definitely drowning."

Estelle was in shock. She didn't feel she was drowning. She felt quite the contrary. Could the dream have been so strong that it took the pain away? The only thing she felt while she was supposedly drowning was peacefulness. Maybe that was the feeling of death?

Something strange had happened, something she couldn't explain. That woman in the corner was looking at her when Taylor erupted before her eyes.

"The woman, she's gone," Estelle said staring at the corner of the bathroom.

"What woman, there's no one here. No one for miles."

She seemed so real.

| 5 |

Monday morning Dan woke up to the worst headache he had had since College. He had fallen asleep on the couch and had drunk a whole bottle of Bourbon. His mouth was as dry as the Mojave Desert. He grabbed his phone as he got up. Three missed calls and a message. He pressed the key to play the message hoping it was Estelle but it was his secretary.

"Hello Dan, the rental place called this morning to set up an appointment for the expert to see the damage caused to the car. Do you know anything about this? Call me back as soon as you get this message."

Dan took a minute to process the information. He rubbed his face and walked to the kitchen to fix himself some coffee. The only way to fight the hangover. He swallowed two pills with his first sip and called his secretary back.

"Hi, just got your message. I have no idea what they are talking about. Did you get his name and number?"

She gave him the information, and he immediately dialed the number anxiously.

"Hi, you called my secretary this morning about a car accident. Could you give me more information about this, please?" Dan asked half-thrilled to finally have some news and half afraid of what the news would be.

"Oh, yes, hello. We got a call from the Sheriff of Blackmont in Montana, reporting a car accident in his jurisdiction. He gave us the license plate, and we ran it through our data and your company's name came up for that rental. We need to send out an expert to evaluate the cost of the damage."

"I understand, do you have any information concerning the driver and the circumstances of the accident?"

"Well, on the file here it says a woman was found in the vehicle. The driver's license they found matches the one we have on file. It seems, the driver was found unconscious."

"Unconscious?" Dan said worriedly.

"Sorry, that's all I have but I could give you the Sheriff's number if you want more details"

"Thank you, that would be very helpful," Dan replied nervously noting the number down and hanging up.

He sat there staring at the number he had just written down, trying to keep his mind focused. When he gathered enough strength he dialed the number.

"Sheriff Allister speaking, how can I help you?"

"Hello Sheriff, I just received a call from my car rental company about an accident that happened in your jurisdiction."

"Oh, yes, may I ask your name?"

"Dan Greenberg, sir, the rental was paid by the company I work for."

"I see, so I presume you know the woman who was driving the vehicle?"

"Yes, if it is Estelle, I know her. We work together. Is she alright?" he asked fearing the response.

"Yes, she is. She was unconscious for a day but has woken up. She seems to be doing fine. She's staying at one of my officer's houses. He is the one who found her on his drive home that night. Her car hit two trees trying to avoid something on the road," Allister explained.

"Thank heavens she's alright," Dan sighed with relief.

"Is it possible to have an address or phone number to reach her?"

"Well, I'll give you a number but forget about coming up here, it's useless for the moment. The roads are blocked with snow for the moment, it's best to wait for a little," Allister said and gave him Taylor's number.

"I understand. Thank you for your help Sheriff."

Dan called his secretary and his boss to tell them what had happened. He then called all the people he had arranged meetings with Estelle to explain and postpone. This took him what was left of his day. He didn't even go to the office. That's what he liked about his job, he could do almost everything from home.

His headache had nearly disappeared when his phone rang.

"Now's not a good time, Linda. Please, can't we just talk about it later?" Dan said to his ex-wife.

"It's never a good time, Dan. That's why we divorced, don't you remember? I need money."

"Ok, how much do you need?" he asked giving up.

"Ten thousand."

"What! Are you kidding me?" he yelled through the receiver as she hung up.

Since the divorce, she had been asking him for money every two or three months, and he couldn't refuse. She was a painter, and if she didn't sell anything she couldn't pay the rent. It was his weak spot. He couldn't leave her like that, so he gave her everything she asked for. He still felt guilty for having ruined their marriage, for never being there. He knew she took advantage of this but it didn't bother him. He hardly spent the money he earned, so he thought he might as well help her out. He connected to his bank online and wired her the amount she had asked for. He didn't call her back. He didn't need to. She knew he would give her the money. All she had to do was ask. They never really had a conversation.

| 6 |

It was past midnight, Taylor was tossing and turning in his bed. He kept thinking about the two incidents. Surely a coincidence, he thought. Estelle was having absences that had already put her in danger two times since the accident. He was going to call Henry first thing in the morning. He couldn't be on the lookout all the time. He kept thinking of her, in fact, he was impatient to wake up the next morning to see her. He enjoyed her company, he hadn't had any in such a long time that he had forgotten what it was like to wake up and have breakfast with someone. He finally fell asleep on those pleasant thoughts.

The house, or more precisely, the cabin, was once again on its own and its inhabitants fast asleep and if you listened carefully enough you'd hear the souls of the house whisper. Before Taylor's grandparents had bought the land and built the ranch, it had been abandoned for years. Luckily, the logs used for the construction were so strong that the cabin had stood undamaged by the work of time and extreme weather. The area itself had been Indian territory, more precisely, home to the Blackfoot Tribe. It was a mystical and sacred place, but they left the area a long time ago.

The most sacred part of their homeland became Glacier National Park in 1910. Taylor's wife was part-Indian, her grandmother was part of the Blackfoot tribe. They had met on his grandparents' land. She had heard so many stories about the place that she'd decided to see for herself. She was a daring and lively person. She wanted to preserve her ancestral tribal history by writing about it. Her research had led her right there and subsequently to Taylor. She was two years older than him and everyone said she had cast a spell on him. They were madly in love with each other. They married young, Taylor was twenty-one. Fate had brought them together and fate had torn them apart. Her name was Koko, which meant «night » in Blackfoot language. She was named like that because she was born during a solar eclipse, on February 26, 1979. Her Blackfoot great-grandmother had chosen that name. Nobody knew it was a Blackfoot name, they just thought it was a reference to Coco Chanel. She had silky dark hair and black pearly eyes. She looked just like her great-grandmother.

After the accident, the bodies couldn't even be buried, the car had burnt down, leaving hardly anything amidst the flames, so Taylor had had a memorial stone made instead, though he never went to it. It all was a distant memory, like a dream, nothing seemed real anymore. It's strange how the past can become as vague as an impressionist painting, where you can only remember the feel of things without remembering them clearly. Things like a fragrance, a sound, a taste will remind you of something strong but you can't remember what it reminds you of.

For the first time since the accident, Taylor had a dream, he dreamt of Koko, she was as real as could be making him follow her. They were by Flathead River. She was leading him somewhere, but he kept losing her, at one point he completely lost her and woke up in a panic. As he came back to himself, he felt something was wrong. He did not know what but deep down inside he knew that dream meant something. Koko always told him dreams were messages from beyond to guide those still on Earth. Taylor did not know what to make of this dream. Where was Koko taking him and why? He tried to return to the dream but the more he tried the less sleep he could get. Half-asleep and still not dreaming, Taylor's sleep was definitely broken when he heard a noise coming from the kitchen. He got up silently and tiptoed to the kitchen. He felt ridiculous when he saw it was only Estelle making coffee.

"Having trouble sleeping too?" he asked her.

"Oh, I didn't hear you come in," she said startled.

"As silent as an Indian," he replied smiling and putting down the baseball bat he had taken along with him in a dark corner, so she didn't see it.

"So what's your excuse?" she asked him.

"Can't sleep. Yours?"

"Same thing."

Taylor didn't mention anything about his dream, but as they sat there he couldn't keep his mind off it. He must've had a strange expression on his face because Estelle asked him if he was feeling alright.

"You look worried," she said.

"Who, me? Naa, just thinking of all the things I've got to do today," he answered hoping she wouldn't ask what those things were because he hadn't the slightest clue.

"Oh, I see. Anything I can help with maybe?"

Taylor shook his head. "Unfortunately not," he said shrugging his shoulders with a false sorry grin.

"I feel useless around here, I've already caused enough trouble & I mean with the accident and the other weird things since that I really am sorry about. I mean you've got a life and I feel I'm keeping you from doing what you have to do."

"You're not bothering me, I'm on vacation, really, it's fine. You shouldn't worry about that. Just rest and those weird things will disappear by themselves. You're just very tired by the shock. It was a traumatic incident, you shouldn't take it for granted. I mean you're just reacting to the fact that you faced death and escaped it. Just feel lucky."

It was the first time Taylor expressed himself so freely with attachment and it was the first time Estelle heard the truth about her accident. The fact that she could have died and was lucky that she was still alive and had no real injuries. Both were surprised by that unique moment. A moment where you feel the slip and are aware of it, a moment when the truth and honesty slip in and takes the floor.

As the words came out of Taylor's mouth the tears started running down Estelle's eyes. She was paralyzed, her heart had stopped beating and her face turned pale. Taylor wrapped his hands around her face and looked into her eyes so as she could read his lips if she wasn't listening.

"Everything's ok now Estelle, you're ok, don't worry."

He put his arms around her, and she nested her head against his chest. She couldn't control the spasms of her crying and the tears kept pouring out of her body. She didn't want him to pull back, she felt safe in his strong arms. She ended up putting her arms around him, and they sat there till what must've been sunrise. The sky still filled with snow, the sun could only be guessed by the hands of the clock. Their embrace was broken by the heavy knocking on the front door. Taylor looked at Estelle puzzled.

"I'm not expecting anyone, especially this early, wait here," he said unwillingly letting go of her to answer the door.

"Sam, wow, what a surprise," Taylor s voice echoed half-worried and half-thrilled as he opened the door.

"Brother, sorry it's been ages, I had to get away, I needed the break, you know," the stranger's voice said slightly shameful.

"Get yourself in here," Taylor said embracing the man in a strong brotherly way.

Estelle could tell the two had been very close despite the clumsy awkwardness of reunions. They didn't know what to say to each other but it was obvious they had a lot to share, they just didn't know how to melt the ice time had built between them.

"Humm, let me introduce you to Estelle," Taylor said scrapping his throat uncomfortably as if he were introducing his mistress to his wife. She's staying here for a while, long story, we'll get to it," he managed to say with a smile.

"Pleasure to meet you, Estelle, I'm Samuel, Taylor's brother-in-law," he said stretching his arm towards her for a handshake.

"Pleasure is mine, Samuel," Estelle answered as they shook hands.

"We were about to have breakfast, want to join us, Sam?" Taylor asked to ease up the seemingly tense atmosphere.

"Sure thing, coffee would be great."

They all went into the kitchen as Taylor got busy fixing breakfast. Estelle couldn't help but wonder who this man was. A brother-in-law. She wouldn't have imagined Taylor was married. She hadn't even thought of it. After all, he did seem like a great guy and in a small town like this, it would seem strange if he were single unless he had big problems of some sort. She unwillingly felt jealous, but why would she be jealous? She stared at Sam as Taylor and he started breaking the ice. He was tall, broad-shouldered, and dark-skinned. She liked to think he must have had Indian blood or something. He had a warm smile but something grave came out of his composure, something fierce, sleeping fire, but he also had that dark beauty with his jet black silky hair and deep black eyes able to switch from the warmest feel to anger-filled defiance. They reminded her of an eagle, but she had the impression she had seen those eyes before.

Estelle was starting to feel uncomfortable between both men. She felt her presence was an obstacle to their ice-breaking. She sipped her coffee and swallowed her toast and dismissed herself. Her French politeness made it seem completely natural and unpremeditated. As she left the kitchen she could feel the atmosphere settle down.

She felt she had done the right thing as she entered her room closing the door behind her. The room felt damp and cold, all of a sudden she felt very uncomfortable and didn't know what to do. She walked over to her suitcase to get something warm to wear. All her clothes felt damp. She had shivers running up her spine, and she started feeling sick, so she decided to climb into her bed and crawl underneath the covers. The sweat ran down her forehead, and she was shivering cold. She tried to go to sleep to shake off what seemed like the start of the flu. Not able to find sleep she opened her eyes, and they slowly adapted to the light. She jumped up at the sight of the woman she had seen the day before sitting in the corner of the bathroom looking at her. She shook her head to wake up but nothing changed.

The woman stared at her as if she were waiting for an answer. But there had been no question. Estelle tried to talk but still, no sound managed to escape the borders of her lips. She tried to get out of bed, but she could not move. Her entire body was stiff; she couldn't even feel herself breathe. The woman kept looking at her, her eyes pierced through Estelle as if she were communicating something. She had a strange kind of aura. As Estelle was looking at her she suddenly felt hands upon her face, if she had been able to move she would have jumped and reached towards her face as if to chase away a fly. All of a sudden she felt as if she were being slapped, at the beginning it was mild and gentle and then it grew in intensity until it started hurting a little. Finally, she felt a splash of cold water hit her face and when her eyes could make out past it she saw Taylor and Samuel standing before her, their expressions were full of panic and the sight of them startled her and this time she could move again.

Taylor started wiping her face with the towel he held in his hands, searching for some sign of life inside her eyes but her eyes were blank.

"I don't understand what's wrong with her, I better get Henry over here," Taylor said in a worried tone as if she weren't there.

"You want me to call him so you could keep her company?" Samuel said trying to help but still puzzled about this girl.

"Yeah, that would be great, Sam, thanks, the number's next to the phone in the library."

Samuel ran out to call and Taylor sat next to Estelle and took her hand.

"What's going on?" Estelle's fragile voice broke the silence.

It startled Taylor. He looked at her confused.

"Estelle?"

"Where did the woman go?" Is she okay, she seemed as if she needed something. "Did you help her? " was her answer.

Taylor looked at her wondering if she hadn't had a bad concussion in the accident after all. She was having hallucinations. That was the only explanation.

"What woman Estelle? There's no one here but Sam and I. Are you feeling okay? We were calling you and you didn't answer, just wanted to check up on you since you weren't answering the door we came in and found you sweating and shaking in your bed. I touched your face and you were boiling hot. I tried waking you up and you wouldn't wake up but your eyes were open transfixed in a stare, so I ended up splashing some water on you. It worked, I'm sorry about that but I'm having the doctor come check if you're alright. We might have to take you to the hospital despite the weather but if that's what needs to be done we'll do it."

Estelle stared at him blankly, not understanding what was going on, she had all the pieces scattered around in her mind but none of them made sense. Was she going mad? She wished she had never left and that she had not over-reacted with Dan. It was stupid of her to react that way, like a teenager. After all, she was a grown-up now and Dan was an adult she could have just talked to him the way normal people do. It wasn't that big of an issue. Dan was a civilized person, and they could be honest with each other.

"I really fucked it all up," she said.

"What?" Taylor asked.

"I'm a mess right now, I can't think straight. I'm sorry you have to deal with my being stupid and ending up here on your back. Stuck here when you have a life. That'll teach me to over-react."

"Estelle, calm down, there's nothing for you to be sorry for. Accidents happen." His voice faltered as he said this. "Everything's going to work out with time," he said stroking her hair.

"He's coming straight away," Samuel said rushing back into the room catching his breath from the run.

When Estelle saw Samuel's face again she cried out pointing at him. "You look like that woman, that woman that's been here looking at me, you have the same eyes."

They both looked at her in silence then they exchanged a glance between one another. Samuel made a sign to Taylor not to interfere. He quietly walked over to Estelle and bent his knees so that his face was at the same level as hers.

"What woman?" he asked in a low serene voice.

"I saw her twice. The first time was last night while I was taking a bath and just now when you woke me up. She just sits there and looks at me but I can't talk."

"She just looks at you and doesn't try to talk?"

"She looks at me and I feel she wants to talk but her lips don't move and I hear no sound. Each time I tried to talk nothing came out of my mouth and I couldn't even move."

"Strange," Samuel said lost in his thoughts.

"What does she look like, can you describe her?" Sam asked.

"Sam, what's on your mind?" Taylor said annoyed.

"Let me take care of this, Taylor, please," Samuel said clenching his teeth and looking at Estelle waiting for her to answer his question.

"I don't know, it's strange. I can't really give her an age; she doesn't look old or young. She has your eyes, dark piercing eyes and it seems like she's asking me something but I don't know what it is."

"Sam, leave her alone, can't you see she's tired?" Taylor insisted.

"Alright. Sorry about that," he said to Estelle getting up and giving a sign to Taylor to follow him outside the room.

"What's the matter with you?" Taylor asked once they were both in the living-room.

"I have a strange feeling about this. I just want to make it clear," Samuel answered.

"And what's that strange feeling? You've disappeared for

three years and come here without notice at the crack of dawn you and start putting your nose into some girl's hallucinations. A girl you don't even know. How am I supposed to react?" Taylor said in a half-whispering angry tone.

"Sorry Taylor, I wasn't expecting this. Really, this is not how I wanted it to be. I mean seeing you again. I've missed you so much. I couldn't take it here. My mother's loss, Koko's, and your parents almost all at the same time. It was more than I could take. But two days ago I started having strange dreams. You remember how some of us go out and fast, right?"

"Sure, to have a dream," Taylor said now curious.

"Exactly, so I tried so many times since the accident, it wasn't healthy at all but I had to do it, I needed answers but nothing came. So I stopped and decided to do something different with my life, something useful. I went out to Africa but that's a different story. Well, like I was saying, I've been having strange dreams since Friday, dreams of Koko. She was making me follow her through this place along the Flathead river, remember, where we used to hang out? The point is, I've never had a dream of her, no matter how hard I tried and bam, three years later, out of the blue, she's back. That's what brought me here. I left Africa straight away. I had to see you, I had to be here."

Shivers went up Taylor's spine when Samuel got to the part of his dream, the same dream he had had that morning.

"You alright?" Samuel asked Taylor holding his arm.

"Yeah, it's just that, well that dream of yours with… I had the same one this morning," he said trying to make out the pieces.

They both stared at each other in silence.

"What do you make of this?" Taylor asked.

"Well, there are stories, you know we always have stories. There is one saying that when there is an unnatural death in the family, the spirit of the person could come back in dreams to show what has really happened. Once it is known the spirit may rest in peace. What is strange is that these dreams of Koko are also a stranger's hallucinations," Samuel explained.

"You're thinking that... was killed?" Taylor couldn't say the name and for the first time, his face twisted in pain.

"But how, I mean, it was an accident, why, if what you are saying is real, why would she need to clear things and why would a perfect stranger be involved? It makes no sense."

"It is strange but you have to think the way she did. She never did anything like anyone else. There must be a reason for this," Samuel said firmly.

Estelle couldn't help overhearing the end of their conversation, hidden in the hallway. The entire conversation was the strangest thing Estelle had ever heard. For a long moment silence had invaded the room. Neither one of them tried to break it. Both men were buried in their thoughts, scrapping for memories to figure out what was going on. Trying to find an explanation. Samuel didn't look all that fierce anymore. Estelle tried to imagine what had happened and who they were talking about. She had never seen Taylor look worried before. His whole face had shifted in a way that she could hardly recognize him. The doorbell broke the silence. Estelle snuck back into her bed.

| 7 |

Taylor looked at Samuel. "I know you don't like him, but he's the only doctor who lives close enough to drive through this weather, he's used to it, just like you and me."

"Sure I get it."

Taylor opened the door. "Hey Henry, I hope the drive wasn't too bad. Thanks so much for coming on such short notice again."

"No problem. I've known better conditions but, needless to say, I'm used to it!" he said laughing until his eyes caught sight of Samuel.

"I didn't know you had guests, hello Sam," Henry said coldly.

Sam only answered by waving his hand briefly.

"Yeah, the tide brought him in this very morning. Here, follow me, she's in the bedroom. I'm worried because she's been having quite a few hallucinations since she's been here.

And I don't think it's very normal. I'm worried she might hurt herself," Taylor explained.

Both men walked into the room silently.

"Estelle, Henry's here to see you, he's the doctor."

"Hello doctor," she said shyly.

"Hello Estelle, let's see how you are feeling today," he said coming to her side of the bed.

Samuel entered the room and stood arms crossed beside Taylor, their eyes on Estelle and Henry.

Estelle quickly focused on Henry and his questions. As he sat next to her on the bed and leaned towards her to check her blood pressure and as he approached, she noticed how time had left its mark on each corner of his face. The lines, circles, and cracks around his mouth and eyes did not disserve him. He had a good face, gentle and wise. He seemed to be a happy man.

"So, have you been having any headaches or dizzy spells?" was his first question.

"Just mild ones once in a while, more like I was drowsy," she answered waiting for his reaction.

"Have you experienced nausea?"

"Not really, but I did get dizzy spells, they went away before I even noticed them."

"How's your vision? Does anything feel different? Does light bother you? " he continued.

"A little but it's not unbearable."

"I see," he said as he flashed a light into her pupils.

When the light penetrated her eyes, Estelle slightly convulsed and the woman appeared before her, holding her hand, at the exact spot Henry had been seconds before. Estelle stared at the woman's hand holding hers, but could not feel it. She felt completely numb and could not speak. As the light flashed before her eyes again she had vanished, and Henry reappeared before her cautiously observing her.

"You just lost a little balance there, didn't you?" he observed.

"I don't know, I didn't feel it," she mumbled out and searched for Taylor's eyes, as drops of sweat popped out of her face. At the sight of this Henry frowned and took her temperature.

"Her temperature is low," he said with a puzzled look on his face trying to put the symptoms together.

Estelle was still struggling to make eye contact with Taylor, but he was too absorbed by the look on Henry's face. She noticed he was tense, twisting both of his hands into fists one at a time. His face had changed, not that he had been quite the smiling type but simply relaxed and now he looked preoccupied. She completely ignored Henry, she wasn't at all worried about herself, she felt that something serious, some sort of inner turmoil had slipped into Taylor and Samuel's presence didn't seem as comforting as it had promised to be.

"I think you're right about the concussion. I can't do anything more from here. She needs a screening," Henry said breaking the silence.

Taylor sighed.

"There's no way to get her to the hospital with the snow, the clinic won't be enough if she needs screening but at least I could put her under observation," Henry continued.

Taylor's face twisted, and he hit his hand in his other hand to control himself and started shouting, "Damned place this is, damn snow, damn hills!"

Henry didn't expect such a reaction. He said nothing but his face showed enough that he hadn't seen it coming. He had never seen Taylor act in such a manner.

"I'm sorry Taylor," he managed to say in a low sorry tone.

"Then, let's take her to the reservation," Samuel interrupted.

"They have nothing better there, no offense," Henry said firmly not bothering to look at Samuel.

"We have different ways of doing things," Samuel shot back with a hint of offense in his voice.

Taylor looked at Samuel surprised, he didn't seem to be familiar with that edgy side of him or maybe he had changed during his long absence, or was it Taylor that had changed?

Henry, on the other hand, didn't seem at all surprised by Samuel's reaction and tone.

Estelle's gaze drifted in Samuel's direction as she focused on him, she could see he wasn't going to let go. Something inside him, something instinctive was boiling up and trying to take over. He didn't seem to have much control over his reactions. His eyes fierce this time, like small pebbles, pointing out at Henry, thriving for the confrontation. Henry looked back in Estelle's direction and finally said to who would care to listen. "It's not up to us to decide, it's up to her."

Taylor straightened himself and walked towards Samuel.

"Are you sure?" he asked calmly.

Samuel looked at him straight in the eyes, his love for him, calming his temper down.

"Of course," he answered, his lips hardly moving from the clutch he was holding his jaw in. "There is nothing white medicine can do for her. Trust me."

"I hope you know what you're doing, I trust you," Taylor almost whispered.

Henry got up, and before he left the room, he added, "Well, I guess you know where to reach me if you need anything."

Taylor walked towards Estelle and took her hand in his.

"I saw her again, the woman, when he flashed the light into my eyes," she whispered. "She was holding my hand."

He put his hand to her forehead and stroke her hair.

"It's okay Estelle, don't worry, you'll be fine. Sam is someone that can be trusted," he reassured her.

Estelle still didn't feel worried and left her fate in his hands. This didn't resemble her at all, she was the responsible type, not the crazy type. Why would she trust a perfect stranger, now two of them, instead of a professional doctor? She had no clue. Maybe it would be the stupidest thing she'd ever done but this time she did not care. The curiosity all these situations and mysteries had waken was too great for her to resist. All of it was most intriguing. The life she had before the accident seemed trivial, there was so much more to live right there. She felt like she was stepping into someone else's life, something had changed inside of her as well. She acted as if she had nothing to lose.

"How do you plan on taking her there?" Taylor asked Samuel.

"The same way I came," Samuel shot back with a grin.

Samuel's face had lightened up once Henry had left the room like dark clouds disappearing after the storm. Was there something between them or was it just the satisfaction of winning the battle?

"Which is?" Taylor insisted on the last word his eyes opening wide.

"The creek, don't you remember anything?" Samuel said as if it were obvious.

"Boy, you look different," Samuel added cunningly.

"Not used to seeing you make decisions." Taylor shrugged with a wink.

Samuel moved towards him and playfully hit his shoulder.

"Since when do you talk to that old bastard anyway?" Samuel asked rocking Taylor's shoulder back and forth.

"Sam, you've been gone a long time, I was alone here, things change. Besides, he helped me a lot, so did Tim. They were my parents' friends, remember? I can't see them the same way you do."

Samuel shrugged his shoulders, " If you say so. That explains the police jacket, I guess."

"I better go talk with him before he leaves," Taylor said ignoring Samuel's last remark and realizing Henry was surely in the living-room waiting for him.

"Henry, I'm sorry about all this," Taylor managed to say honestly.

"It's okay, sonny, I didn't know who was calling, he didn't say, so I wasn't prepared to see him around here. It's been such a long time. I forgot how much he hates me," Henry said with regret. "Now, I just don't want the girl to develop any serious symptoms, but we do have a situation here with this damn weather. I understand your concern, I'm sorry I can't be more helpful. Make sure she gets a lot of rest and keep a note of any strange thing she does. I think she's having small seizures, concise ones, she can hardly notice them herself. They could be just post-traumatic reactions and disappear with time but if they don't then that's a more serious issue, and she'll have to go to a hospital," he concluded on this, patted Taylor's back, and left.

Taylor now realized the comfortable world he had been living in was falling apart piece by piece, but what else could he expect for having shut away so many emotions and acting as if nothing had ever happened. The reality was bound to slap him back in the face at some point, and there it was. That point was now. Although he was expecting it to happen he never thought it would be with so much relief.

He hadn't felt quite himself in such a long time that the rebirth was invigorating. He felt all the energy he had been wasting, to shut everything out the moment he learned Sam had left, fill him anew. From that moment on, he started living in a cage, a cage devoid of emotions, he did this because he didn't want to be angry against Sam. Sam and he were very close, and he took his departure very personally, but deep down he could not blame Sam because Sam did what Taylor had not dared to do. He didn't want to be angry because he knew Sam wasn't letting him down, Sam saw the world and things differently, on the more spiritual ground. Taylor could not blame him for that even though it would have been easier to be angry and let go.

| **8** |

The phone was ringing.

"Hello," said the voice.

"Hi, am I speaking to Taylor?" Dan asked politely.

"Yes, may I ask who's calling?" Taylor replied.

"Hi Taylor, I'm sorry to bother you, I'm Dan, Estelle's friend. Sheriff Allister gave me your number, so I could speak to her."

Dan's voice caved into Taylor's ears, he didn't like the sound of his voice nor the way he spoke.

"Oh, I see, are you a family member?" Taylor asked.

"No, I'm her manager and friend. Is she doing okay?"

"Yes, she's fine, but she's very tired, the doctor just left, and she fell asleep. She's been getting a lot of rest," Taylor explained.

"Thank Heaven she's okay. From what I've been told it was a nasty accident, and she was lucky. You're the one who found her, right?"

"Yeah, she is lucky, it was a close call. If the car had pushed a little further she would have ended up in the ravine," Taylor answered with his serious police tone.

"Thank you for looking after her, I'll try calling back later."

"No problem. Do you want me to leave her a message or something?"

"Sure, tell her I was worried because I couldn't get her on the phone. I wish I could come up there but the Sheriff told me the roads were blocked for the moment. Oh yes, and tell her not to worry about work, for now, I've postponed all our engagements and everyone was more than understanding. Also, tell her I'm sorry, she'll know why."

"Ok Dan, I'll give her the message when she wakes up. Thanks for calling and we'll keep in touch," Taylor said in a kind and professional voice.

"Thanks, Taylor, keep in touch."

Dan hung up and put the phone down. The short conversation had emptied him. The day had been long and emotionally tiring. He served himself a glass of wine, red wine, the only real wine according to him. It was a bottle of Pinot Noir, his favorite. He sat down, made himself comfortable, and turned the TV on. He hadn't watched the news since the night of the argument with Estelle. Time had somehow evaporated with all the stress he had piled up these past few days. Relaxing was a little easier now that he knew where Estelle was and that she was alright but it wasn't enough for him to totally relax. Something new was bothering him, this Taylor.

Dan felt proud to be the only person Estelle really knew, he felt in control. He loved to feel in control. Things were somehow different now and it annoyed him. He wondered if she were still angry after him, after what had happened. Maybe she was and didn't want to talk to him, maybe this guy lied about the fact that she was sleeping, maybe she had told him to say that if he'd called? He grabbed the phone to give it another try but pride stopped him. He noticed Spencer had tried to call him five times, he knew Spencer would be pissed at him, and he did not want to deal with it for now. The only thing he could think of now was Estelle.

He'd never been to Montana, who would want to go there anyway? Sure the landscape must be breath-taking but apart from that what else was there to do out there? Dan was the real city type guy. Nothing could make him take a peaceful retreat. He tried once with Linda, his ex-wife, she loved nature, of course, since she was a painter. She took him to Yosemite once. He hadn't been able to sleep the entire time they were there. Too much silence, Dan needed noise. Silence killed him, stressed him out more than anything. The nights were endless and the days were boring. He wasn't the outdoor type either. The only outdoors he liked were bars, clubs, and restaurants. He had been a pain that entire stay and Linda never asked him to go with her again. Needless to say, Dan never argued it. Come to think of it, Dan and Linda had never shared much, they both led their own separate lives. Linda would have wanted someone she could tag along in all her extravagances but Dan was not one to make efforts.

His work was the most important thing, nothing else counted. Of course, he had friends, work friends, or people who wanted to keep him handy just in case. He was good at what he did, helping young artists come to light, that's why Spencer would never get rid of him. Dan was rough in business and if something bothered him he'd get rid of it. His enemies in the business were countless but paradoxically it served him well. People knew better than to fool around with him, they knew they wouldn't get away with it easily. Because of his harsh reputation, Dan had trouble finding artists who weren't reluctant to work with him so he started looking for foreign artists. That's how Estelle arrived in his catalog.

Dan had given up trying to concentrate on the news and kept on drinking wine, thoughts kept popping into his mind one after the other, and he had lost all hope of relaxation for the night. So he let the wine do the trick. He finished the entire bottle as he sat there looking at the pictures moving on the screen in front of him and finally fell asleep.

| 9 |

The cold air whipped Taylor's face as he stepped outside to take care of Shakespeare. All his prospects had now been completely challenged by the turn of events. Events he would never even have imagined. Taylor's mind hadn't been so consumed in years. He needed to clear it up. Before he knew it he had saddled up and was riding Shakespeare out into the snow. What had been a pond was now a giant piece of ice and the peaceful feeling the snow brought was indescribable. Taylor took it all in, in one big breath, his eyes closed. It felt like riding through cotton.

At least he had found someplace where time had managed to stand still, out there no human could get a grip on nature's plans. He let Shakespeare take his favorite trail and sat back to enjoy the moment, but the dream he had had about Koko kept breaking into his thoughts. He tried as hard as he could to ignore it but it forced itself in and even the cold couldn't numb his thoughts enough to make it disappear. The snow kept on falling, he could not see very far and each time he exhaled a huge cloud of smoke blurred his vision even more. His mind was playing tricks on him, he knew it, Koko was sometimes behind a tree showing him a path, so he tried to follow her but once he approached the tree close enough there would be no one there. At other times the wind would whisper her faint and almost inaudible voice. His head started spinning, and he was lost in thought, not paying attention to time nor distance.

The ride, the air, and the cold were like a drug he was addicted to, he let the horse carry him away regardless. Such an unusual high that he abandoned himself willingly in. His fingers had already stiffened with the freezing air penetrating through the layers of wool and leather. Each breath he took pinched his chest, but he never turned back. At this point his mind was numb, his entire body seemed numb, he was relieved from feeling anything he did not want to feel. But at what price? His eyes filled with tears he could not control, his throat tightened and his chest froze as a loud screeching scream forced its way out of Taylor and into the silent frozen air.

It seemed and felt as though it went on forever and the echo of it continued through the endless mountains and sky around him. Shakespeare turned back on his own and headed for the stable. Taylor was knocked out and he drifted away. When he came back to himself he was still on Shakespeare but in the stable. He managed to step down but he felt intoxicated. His legs were weak and shaky. His heart was thumping and his brain was dazed. He walked back into the house and straight to his room. He undressed and headed to the bathroom to take a warm bath.

At first, the warmth of the water hurt his limbs. His hands had almost been frost-bitten. He slowly tried to move them but it hurt and burned. He could not make out the different sensations of the freeze and the burn. He finally put his head back and relaxed. Letting every inch of his body recuperate from the icy ride. His eyes closed and his muscles relaxed, the visions of Koko crept back into his head. He shook his head to make them disappear. Once his eyes were open he could not relax any longer. He had to go check up on Estelle. Before he returned to see Estelle he gathered his thoughts and spirits. He had to be composed and comforting, she needed to feel safe. She had enough to deal with right now.

He hardly knew her, but he felt her, he felt she was lost, he felt she was looking for something, something to fill the void, to find a meaning to her life. He wondered what had brought her here and when would be the next time someone would drop into his life like that, unexpected. She was a sign, a sign of change, of redemption maybe. He had mourned in his manner way for years, he had in some sort died his own slow death. He hadn't been living, he had been hiding from life. Nothing made him want to live, but Estelle, something in her made him want to live. He felt important, he felt necessary.

Was she the missing piece of the puzzle? Isn't life a puzzle, aren't we all looking for the pieces? Sometimes you don't see the right piece and it's right there in your hand, you go through all the other ones, one by one, time flies and at the end, you look down to see what you were looking for all this time was right there in front of you, in the palm of your hand and you think how stupid you were. How obvious can obvious be? When you don't want to see it or when you're not ready to, it mysteriously disappears.

| 10 |

Samuel's dark eyes had been staring at Estelle for a while. If he had been able to penetrate her mind and soul through her eyes he would already have seen everything there was to see. His stare started to make her feel uncomfortable as if he could read in her every thought. It felt as if she lay naked before him. His insisting study of her every move and reaction had finally forced her to stay perfectly still, defying him.

"Don't worry, I'm not going to hurt you," his new gentle voice murmured.

Estelle was surprised by his tone, it was soft and caring, unlike the other times she had heard him speak. She suddenly realized she was holding his hand and squeezing it tightly.

"Sorry if I'm intruding, but how did you get here? Taylor told me there had been a car accident," he questioned.

Estelle nodded. "Yes, I don't remember much, in fact, I don't remember anything about the accident," she said avoiding.

"I see. Do you remember what you were thinking about just before the crash?" he asked.

"Well, as I said, I don't know, I don't remember crashing," her voice shrieked on the last word.

"I know you remember Estelle. I won't tell anyone, trust me," he insisted.

She cringed, her back stiffened, and she loosened her grip, ripping her hand away from his and biting her upper lip.

"No you don't!" she yelled tears swelling up her eyes. "Who do you think you are anyway, calling me a liar? Do you think I like this situation? Do you really think I'm happy stuck here in the middle of nowhere with perfect strangers making me feel like I'm going mad or something?" she cried out her hands shaking and tears choking her from time to time. Her breathing was loud and difficult.

"Now, now, Estelle, please, calm down. I mean no harm. Really, I simply want to help you. I'm not accusing you of anything, I'm just trying to make your memories resurface," he said trying to calm her down. He took her in his arms until her breathing slowed down and became more natural.

"I don't want to remember," she admitted.

Samuel sighed and tightened his embrace.

"I know it's hard, I know it's easier to shut things out rather than face them. But it only lasts a while, if you hold everything in it will haunt you longer. Your visions mean something, Estelle. You see, where I come from, we believe in the supernatural. My people have to go and fast for days before they could have the kind of dream you had. It's not given to everyone, only a few chosen ones get to have these dreams."

Estelle remained quiet, her head still nested in his arms.

"That's why we must know what you were thinking of before you crashed," he continued in a slow and low voice so that she could catch the meaning of every word.

She then raised her head away from his chest and looked at him blankly not knowing what to make of this conversation.

"My family has fasted many times since Koko's death to find an answer but nothing ever came to anyone. Not one sign, not one dream, not one song. This is the very first time Koko reappears. You see, no one in the tribe believed her death was an accident, so we've been searching for explanations ever since."

"What makes you so sure that these visions of mine are related to this Koko you're talking about?" she managed to ask without over-reacting.

"It's something you said earlier today, when I walked into the room, you said the woman you had been seeing had the same eyes as me. Koko was my elder sister and Taylor's wife. See, we had the same eyes, we had our grandmother's eyes."

Estelle said nothing but was trying to fit the pieces together in her head. This woman, was she real or just her imagination? Yet every time this apparition came she was numb and in danger of death. She tried to remember what she was thinking of before the accident, but she couldn't. Her anger against Dan being too present to put it aside from any other preoccupations she might have had. She continued digging each corner of her memory but it quickly made her feel tired. She felt her skull caving in on her brain and forcing her to stop rummaging. Her eyelids felt heavy and she finally surrendered to sleep. Samuel tried not to move in fear of waking her up. He thought that maybe she would see Koko again and this time he would be next to her. He watched her sleep.

"Sam? Is she alright?" Taylor asked in a low voice.

Sam nodded. "I think so, she's really tired," he answered still looking at her for any hint of disturbance.

"Has anything new happened?"

"No, nothing, she just fell asleep," Sam reported and looked up at Taylor.

"You really should be getting some rest as well, you look like hell. I'll stay up and watch over her," Sam suggested.

Taylor scratched his head and agreed, " I'll just fix myself something to eat before, you want anything?"

"No, I'm fine, I can wait. That breakfast was more than I can handle," Sam said smiling.

"Okay, help yourself whenever you feel like it. You're home here," Taylor said leaving the room.

"Hey, could you turn the light off please?" Sam asked.

"Sure."

The room was dark even though it wasn't very late, it must have been around 5:30 pm or something. The snow had totally frozen over the windows and the wind was blowing hard. A tree branch was scraping the wall outside with each gust of wind and with each snowflake sticking to the layer of ice on the window the sound of the wind deafened and turned the room into a warm womb. The whistle of the wind sounded like faint human voices flying by and fading away.

Samuel was not afraid of spirits, he had been brought up in a culture that believed and accepted them to live amongst them. He believed in evil ones and good ones. He felt nothing evil around him, there was a feeling of safety, he wasn't worried, Estelle was in no danger, Koko wouldn't do her any harm. Koko was a good person, everyone who knew her loved her. She was that kind of person, the kind would you always remember, the kind you would turn around to look at when she came into a room. She had that aura. She drew respect. Although she was exceptionally beautiful from the outside, her soul was also beautiful. She did a lot for her people, for the reservation. Even as a child she had that special something and so much energy. The gift of feeling people's grief and helping them.

Although Samuel missed her a lot he did not feel sad, the anger he had felt after the accident had faded away, but he still hadn't found complete peace, something was missing, maybe her body, it would have been easier if the bodies had been identified and with a real burial? He could feel her spirit; he could feel she wasn't at peace the minute he had walked onto Taylor's premises.

Samuel felt as if he had never left the area. What had become only but a vague memory had splashed back into his entire being. This was his home, where he grew up, where he became who he was. So much time he had tried to find himself, he thought Africa was where he belonged, but he realized he also could help there in his roots, just like Koko had done. Helping his people. Sitting there in the silent dark room, these thoughts crept into his mind and things became clearer, more meaningful. He almost felt ashamed of himself for being so selfish in leaving everyone behind. But if he hadn't left he probably wouldn't have been aware of it. It was his journey and experience that brought him to this, and Koko had brought him back where he belonged. Where he could fulfill all she hadn't had the chance to.

| 11 |

Taylor was awakened by a ray of sunshine upon his eyes, the night had been peaceful. Once his eyes adapted to the sunlight they hadn't seen in days, he jumped out of bed and ran to the window. The sky was as blue as a turquoise, not the slightest cloud. The snow on the window had started to melt but was now a thick transparent layer of ice. Taylor was feeling light-hearted and excited. He felt like he had been sleeping for years and that he had just woken up. Everything had the feel of something new and special. He had the feeling something good was about to happen.

He thought of his guests and how good it was to have them under his roof to share breakfast with. The thought of it thrilled him, he threw himself under a hot shower and dressed quickly, then paced to the kitchen humming across the house. As he walked to the kitchen, he observed the sun penetrating from every window giving a church-like feel to the house. It all felt very spiritual, very soothing. He stopped to take in all the energy the warm light was giving him, he soaked it all in and took a long and deep breath.

Estelle opened her eyes and searched the room to find out where the noise was coming from but what she found was Samuel fast asleep by her side. She stared at him, the sun reflecting on his golden skin. She fought the urge of caressing his cheek, he looked so peaceful. Then she focused on the noise again, it was coming from the kitchen. She delicately got up and left the room being as quiet as possible, doing her best not to wake Samuel up. She tiptoed through the hallway and stopped still in the living-room admiring the beauty of the place with the sun's rays streaming in and dancing around. She reached the kitchen and saw Taylor, he was beaming, she was surprised to see the contrast from how he was yesterday. His eyes met hers and they both smiled.

"Looks like someone got a good night's rest!" he said to her.

"I could say the same for you!" she answered blushing.

"Have you seen Sam?" Taylor asked suddenly remembering he was supposed to keep an eye on her.

"Yeah, he's still asleep, I did my best not to wake him up. He was sound asleep," Estelle said picturing Samuel's peaceful face.

"So, no nightmares or sleep-walking this time?" he teased.

"I slept like a baby. I'm starving, what are you cooking?"

"Scrambled eggs, bacon, and toast. Hey Sam, how's it going?"

"Not bad at all, starving too," he said with a radiant smile perfectly aware he had startled Estelle by his unexpected closeness.

"I didn't even hear you come in," she said all surprised.

"Better get used to it, it's one of his many talents," Taylor grinned proudly of his joke.

They all sat around the table and had breakfast talking about the end of the snowstorm and their plans for the day. Estelle listened to them more than she spoke. She admired how quickly the complicity between both men had come back as if they had never been separated. The heavy atmosphere that had settled in yesterday was but a mere memory as if it had been a dream. After all, was Estelle's memory playing tricks on her, maybe she had dreamt it all?

"You promised I could go for a ride once the snow stopped," Estelle said vividly interrupting their conversation.

Both men looked at each other puzzled.

"Estelle, I'd love to let you ride but you heard the doctor yesterday, you need to rest, riding is not a good idea," Taylor said softly.

Estelle nodded and knew that yesterday hadn't been a dream but how could today feel so different?

What could have made such a situation change in one night? She felt like she had missed out on something. Taylor and Samuel seemed so different, so serene and joyful, not the worried and angry people they had been yesterday. She sat back in the chair and observed them trying to dig up any memory that could explain this sudden change but nothing came. The more she focused the more her head caved in on her until she felt faint and Taylor helped her back into her bed.

"See, you need to rest some more, I know it's no fun being locked up in here with nothing to do but there's nothing else to do for now," Taylor said pulling the covers over her so that she could fall asleep.

"How's your head? Is it aching or anything?"

Estelle shook her head and closed her eyes to abandon herself to sleep.

A car was pulling up into the driveway, Taylor went to the door and made out Tim's patrol car.

"Hey, Sheriff!" Taylor yelled out.

"Hey sonny, just thought I'd stop by to see how everything was going," Tim said climbing up the stairs to the porch and shook his boots before he entered the house.

"The sun's back but it's still freezing, I tell you. I could sure use a nice warm cup of coffee," Tim said taking his coat off and walking towards the kitchen with Taylor.

"Coffee right away sir," Taylor said rushing into the kitchen.

"Sam's back, he just got here yesterday."

Both Samuel and Tim remained polite and greeted each other from a distance.

"I better be getting ready," Samuel said, getting off his chair and out of the kitchen.

"So how's the girl?" Tim asked in a more serious tone.

"She's okay, Henry came to check up on her yesterday, and

she might have to go to the hospital if her symptoms don't improve. She's really tired," Taylor explained.

Tim started talking about the phone call he had had from Dan and asked if he had called Taylor. They both agreed on the fact that he must be a west coast showoff. They didn't really appreciate the way he talked to them. Not the kind of people they were used to around there.

"He might be showing up here sometime soon since the snowstorm is over," Tim concluded.

"I guess so, I'm surprised she's never mentioned him nor anyone else. In her place, I would have called my family and friends to let them know I was okay," Taylor went on.

"Who knows, maybe she was running away from something or someone. Who in their right mind would drive up here at this time of the year without the proper equipment? She didn't even have chains on her damn car. I mean, no wonder she crashed, even if there hadn't been something which had caught her off guard, it was bound to happen. I saw she was using a GPS, you know what I think about those damn things, DANGEROUS. Did she mention anything at all?" Tim said still lost in his thoughts.

"Not a thing, she won't talk about it. She says she doesn't remember anything."

"Maybe it's true or maybe she's hiding something. I'll talk to her when she feels better."

"I'll give you a call."

"Thanks. You didn't mention Sam was coming back." Tim finally tackled the subject.

"I didn't know, he showed up at the door at the crack of dawn yesterday morning."

"What was he up to all this time?"

"I don't really know yet. We haven't had a chance to sit down and talk yet with Estelle being here and all. It's been quite intense," Taylor explained.

"Well, guess that's good news for you. You two were real close," Tim said tapping Taylor's shoulder in a fatherly way.

"Yeah, it was a bit of a shock to see him, but I'm really happy that he's back."

"Good, alright sonny, got to head back, work to do. People are going to start calling me now that the sun is back," he said as he finished the coffee, put his hat back on, and walked out of the kitchen.

"Ok, let me know of anything new," he yelled out as he hopped into his car and started the engine.

Taylor waved at him as he watched him pull out of the driveway slowly.

"The old man's not getting any younger, but he seems to have smoothed out a little, I have got to admit," Samuel's voice surprised Taylor by its closeness.

Samuel giggled when he saw that his voice had startled Taylor.

"Damn it, Sam, don't do that, I'm not used to it anymore!" he said softly punching Samuel in the stomach.

They both started to fight playfully, their laughter filled the room.

"I hope I'm not interrupting anything," Estelle's voice

echoed shortly followed by childish giggles. They blushed when they pictured the situation. They had been fighting like little boys in the schoolyard.

"No please, don't mind me, I'm just going to go out for a little walk, get some fresh air," she said.

"Are you sure? It's really freezing, don't trust the sunshine. You're not dressed warm enough to go out," Taylor insisted.

"I really could use the fresh air," she pleaded.

"Ok, put this on and we'll come with you," Samuel said handing her the big leather coat that was on the hanger.

Estelle grabbed it gently and put it on while both men put their shoes and coats on.

The place was beautiful, the snow-covered mountains were breathtaking, they walked for what seemed to be a long time. Taylor and Samuel commented on the surroundings like guides. Estelle listened to every word and was fascinated like a child in a toy store. Her eyes caught sight of a majestic elk, she tried to approach it slowly but Samuel and Taylor laughed. As soon as the elk saw her it turned around and gracefully ran off in the opposite direction. She watched it disappear into the trees and the snow when something else caught her attention. She felt she was being watched and something was pulling her closer into a path off the main trail they had been walking on.

Samuel and Taylor had started a snowball fight when she decided to see where she would be taken to. The lights and shadows underneath the massive trees danced with the sun's rays. Suddenly she thought she had heard someone whisper her name. She shivered and stood still to concentrate on the different sounds surrounding her. Nothing else.

A second later her eyes met the woman's eyes. She was standing arms stretched along her body graciously. Standing there in the snow, under those trees, she looked like what believers would call an angel. Her complexion was pale and the long dark hair was floating in the air as if she had been immersed in water. The waves of hair were hypnotizing. Her feet didn't even seem like they touched the ground. Estelle stared at her bewildered and in admiration. It was a beautiful sight to see. The woman's lips did not move but Estelle heard the whispers again.

"Don't lose yourself, follow the way," sang out the voice.

Estelle tried to approach the woman but the moment her foot rose from the ground the woman vanished.

"There you are! We've been looking for you, you shouldn't go off the trail, there could be hunting traps," Taylor yelled out a few yards away.

"Sorry, I thought I had seen someone, I mean something… the elk. I wanted to see it up close. " she stuttered still trying to understand what she had just seen. She decided to keep this to herself. She didn't want to be taken to the hospital. She slowly walked back to the trail, and they all agreed it was high time they started walking back to the house.

They had been walking for quite some time, it was early afternoon when they caught sight of the house and a shiny red car.

"You expecting anyone?" Samuel asked Taylor.

"Not that I know of," Taylor answered trying to make out the license plate.

Estelle's heart sank to the ground. She couldn't believe it, Dan's car. She felt upset, she didn't want to see him, not here, not now. She seriously considered pretending she was amnesiac, but she didn't feel she feared she would not be able to pull it off and get away with it. Not with Dan. As they got closer Estelle realized it wasn't Dan's car. All the weight that had oppressed her melted out on the spot.

"May I help you?" Taylor asked as he knocked on the car window.

The man hadn't seen them coming and was surprised. He immediately opened the door, stepped out of the car and presented his hand to Taylor, and introduced himself.

"Hello, I'm David Turner, the expert from the insurance company, you must be Taylor?"

"Oh, I see, yes Sheriff Allister told me you would be coming along to see the car," Taylor answered as he accepted to shake his hand.

"Missus Lenoir, I presume," David said looking at Estelle.

"Nice to meet you," she said in a shy voice.

"I didn't expect you to come so soon," Taylor continued.

"Well, I've been waiting at the hotel in town for the storm to clear. Could you take me to the car?"

"Sure. Sam, could you fix Estelle something to eat while I take care of this. I'll be back soon."

"Will do."

"I want to come too," Estelle said.

"I don't think it's such a good idea," Taylor said his eyes searching for help from Samuel.

"Maybe we should all go," Samuel disagreed with Taylor.

"I'll drive," Taylor said upset.

Estelle and Samuel sat in the back while David sat next to Taylor. The engine roared and Johnny Cash's voice filled the car. No one spoke. When the car started backing up Estelle clutched the seatbelt and the side handle so hard her hands turned red. Samuel placed his hand on hers, and she relaxed at his contact. Taylor noticed her nervousness as he observed her through the rear-view mirror and drove slowly. Ten minutes later he pulled over and parked behind Estelle's car. The car was covered with snow.

"No wonder I didn't see it when I drove up," David said looking at the white pile.

"I'm not sure how you're going to inspect the car," Taylor said skeptically.

They all stepped out of the car and walked to Estelle's car. There was no sign of an accident at first glance. No one could have guessed. Once the men scraped the snow off the car Estelle stared at the crushed hood making one with two tree trunks and the ravine a little further. It all flashed back to her, she was lost, the GPS couldn't find any satellite reception because of the storm. She was struggling to find the heater to defrost the windshield and her stereo was blasting Stone Temple Pilots. " All in the Suit that you Wear" when huge headlights blinded her as the car was trying to avoid a woman crossing the road, she crushed the breaks and the car went swinging to the right, and she blacked-out. It all happened so fast. She felt Samuel's hand on her shoulder.

"Everything okay, Estelle?" he whispered to her ear. "They're finished, we're going back," he said leading her back to Taylor's car.

When they returned to the house, Taylor and Samuel went to the kitchen to prepare something for their late lunch while the expert finished talking to Estelle. She explained she did not remember anything, and he concluded by saying he was going to see with the rental company and with Dan directly. Estelle accompanied him back to the front door and shook his hand. As she closed the door she thought about Dan. What was he going to think about her not calling him at least to tell him she was okay?

She knew he would be worried. She had never left Washington and by now he must have learned that she had emptied the apartment and had had an accident. She dreaded his reaction. Would he be pissed off or would he blame himself? Either way, the situation did not make her feel comfortable. Things seemed so unreal that normal things didn't come to her. Why hadn't she even called her parents to tell them what had happened? Even if she didn't want to speak to Dan she could at least have called his secretary. But she hadn't even thought of doing these things.

It felt like time had stood still as if she were living in some sort of parallel dimension. She hadn't been or felt the same since the accident, but she liked it. She felt comfortable with this strange situation. All her life had been so dull until now. Even the move to Seattle felt dull compared to this. The excitement she had for so long found in the music felt as if it were fading away. She hadn't been able to write a decent song in years. All her good songs were written when she was but a teenager. This frightened her more than she was willing to admit. So her being here in Seattle with Dan fighting for her so-called talent felt fake. What would happen if she wasn't able to write enough good songs for this new album, how stupid would that look?

Dan was overly intense about her talent, he believed in her a lot and placed the bar extremely high. Estelle had trouble coping and identifying in that image of her as an artist. In all the selling herself thing. She wasn't convinced in herself at all. She was only twenty-five, but she felt worn out and emptied. Since she left Paris and her circle of friends, this feeling did nothing but intensify. The more she worked with Dan the more she felt insecure in what was building up. She could only focus on the moment she would have already worked on all her good songs and when Dan would find out she had gone dry, dry out of inspiration, emptied the well.

Thinking of all this Estelle swallowed her pride and tried to focus. Now she had to talk to Dan and call her parents.

She couldn't just sit back and let go of everything she had so dearly been working for all these years. She dialed her parent's number, it rang, and when she heard the answering machine, she left a message saying everything was alright and that she would call them back later. She hung up and was happy that she ended up just leaving a voicemail. She looked at the phone and couldn't get herself to call Dan. It would be so awkward to talk to him after what had happened, she wasn't ready for it. Maybe she could scribble something through email, polite and professional. After all, he was her boss. She walked to her room to get her Blackberry but quickly remembered she had no network. She threw her Blackberry back into her purse, scratched her head trying to think of another solution. She hadn't seen a computer in the house or maybe it was in Taylor's room, maybe a laptop? She then stared at her guitar case next to her suitcase.

"Everything ok?" Sam asked his head hanging from outside the door.
"Sure, let me guess, lunch is ready," she said smiling.
"Good guess!"

Samuel's smile melted all of Estelle's worries away, there was a protective warmth about him, different from Taylor's. There was a whole different dimension to Samuel, she couldn't quite explain how or why. Something about him triggered respect and some sort of admiration, not the way Dan did either. She followed him into the kitchen where she saw Taylor's joyful look, all proud of what he was about to serve.

"Hey, just in case you're a little homesick, here's a French dish. I had a lot of cheese and some white wine and I thought you might be happy," he said all excited.

"Wow, is that a fondue? I can't believe you made that," she said suspiciously staring at the thick paste-like substance that was in the pan he held out for her to see.

"Looks good, doesn't it? I've never made it before but I had a recipe left from my grandmother. It does seem a little thick though, I don't know if it's supposed to be like that."

Estelle looked at the bottle of wine that had barely been touched. "You didn't put enough wine," she said walking over to the stove to grab the bottle and poured almost all its contents into the pan.

"Hey, watch out!" Taylor cried out.

"Don't worry, the alcohol will evaporate, you're supposed to put in a lot of wine," she reassured him. "See, now it'll be easier to dip the bread," she said mockingly.

They all sat at the table staring at the big pot of fondue. Samuel looked at it suspiciously waiting to see how Estelle would serve herself. He was surprised when she just dipped several pieces of toasted bread into the pot and put them on her plate. Estelle giggled at him and told him to try. In the end, they had all enjoyed the dish and the red wine except for Samuel who didn't drink any alcohol. They all laughed as Taylor and Samuel shared their old memories while dipping their last pieces of bread struggling to get the chewy cheese stuck at the bottom of the pot.

"So what is it you're here for? I mean in the US. If I lived in France, I'd probably stay there," Samuel asked Estelle.

"For work," Estelle answered caught off guard.

"And what kind of work?"

"I'm in the music business, I'm a singer-songwriter," she answered anxiously to drop the subject.

"No way, that sounds nice!" Samuel said all excited and not at all willing to change the subject even though he did feel her hesitation. "What kind of music?"

"Rock."

"Cool! Anything we could listen to?" he went on curiously.

Taylor listened to the conversation and wondered why he hadn't thought of asking her these questions himself. He hated what he had become, so uninterested, so indifferent about others and their lives not to forget his own. He did not want to be that person anymore, that person had become a stranger to him since Estelle crashed into his life. It would take a little time for him to lose all his habits and return to the person he once had been. Samuel's return would help in his recovery.

He couldn't believe he had wasted three years of his life just like that. It was pathetic and it ate his heart out. Nothing of his inner turmoil showed on the outside, he had built the strongest carapace that he even managed to fool himself into being alright. Samuel and Estelle continued their talk about music, the bands, and artists they loved, what it was like to write, record, and perform songs. They couldn't guess what Taylor was going through sitting right there between them.

"Wow, you guys had a band?" Estelle cried out putting her hand on Taylor's.

Taylor pulled out of his thoughts surprised and uncomfortable.

"Well, that was a very long time ago," he said embarrassed.

"Yeah, he had let his hair grow to his elbows, and he sang Alice in Chains songs. It was really awful, trust me!" Samuel chuckled.

"Yeah, I know, I know, that's why I gave up pretty fast," Taylor laughed at himself.

"I think it lasted several months, tops."

"Good times," they both said.

Estelle laughed trying to picture them rocking out. It didn't fit them at all. In fact, she couldn't even picture them as teenagers. She knew so many people who wanted to be in rock bands when they were teenagers, they all pretty much quit once in high-school. Many of them still talked about those times with regret and nostalgia. Some of the people she had played with had quit bands because of school. Saying they had no more time for that kind of thing, that music was just a pastime, a hobby not a real job, their parents' pressure being the major reason for it all. So when those friends kept saying how lucky she was to still be in the music and that they wish they were in her place, she just ignored them. Everyone has a choice, no matter what. Some choose comfort and security, others fight for their desires no matter how hard it could be.

Taylor started clearing the table and Estelle joined in to help, and they washed the dishes still talking about different things while Samuel prepared coffee and went out to get more wood for the fireplace. They all drank their coffee in the living room next to the fire. It was already dark outside; they had finished lunch quite late. Silence had filled the room for some time now.

All three were lost in their thoughts again staring into the fire. As Estelle watched the fire dancing she remembered what she had seen that morning in the woods. That strange but beautiful vision, she tried to remember what the whispers she had heard had said. Something about not losing and following something. But what did it mean, was it addressed to her or someone else? What did she have to lose, her chance to make a living with her passion or something deeper, something she felt since she'd woken up in this very house? Which feeling should she follow, the reasonable one or the unexplainable one?

"Estelle, Estelle, hello, do you hear me?" Taylor shouted out to her.

"Yes, sorry, I was day-dreaming?"

"Telephone call for you, a certain Dan," Taylor said.

"Dan?" the deception showed all over her face.

"Do you want me to say you're not available?" Taylor suggested when he saw her reaction while his hand was covering the receiver.

"No, I guess I should talk to him," she finally said not very enchanted by the idea as she walked over to the phone and took it unwillingly from Taylor's hands.

"Hi Dan," she said with a trembling voice.

"Estelle, I'm so glad to hear your voice. You have no idea what I've been through," Dan said.

"I'm sorry, really I am, I just," she stopped, she didn't know what to say.

"It's okay Estelle, the important thing is that you're safe," he said waiting for a reaction. "I've spoken to Spencer, everything is okay, I've talked to everyone and put our engagements to later, they are all more than understanding, and wish that you get better soon. Estelle are you still there?"

"Yes, Dan, I'm here. I just don't know what to say except thank you and I'm sorry, I'm sorry about my reaction. It was childish," she murmured.

"Can't change the past honey, we have to move on and think of the future," he said in a professional tone. "Are you alright where you are or do you want me to do something about it?" he questioned.

"I'm great here, people couldn't be nicer and the place is beautiful, I actually love it here. It's breathtaking."

"Ok, I'll call on you tomorrow. Take care and get better quickly, so I can come and get you. We've got a lot of work to do!"

"Got it. Thanks."

Estelle hung up and stared at the phone. She didn't want to leave; she didn't want to get better even though she wasn't feeling sick or anything. Everyone kept telling her she needed rest when the only thing she needed was life.

| 13 |

The cold penetrated through her every pore and her body stiffened the instant she opened her eyes to find herself at the exact same spot she had seen the woman floating in the woods that very afternoon. She examined herself to see that she was wearing nothing but her nightgown and that she was barefoot in the snow. The glacial wind slashed her skin, and she shivered from head to toe. She started gasping at each breath she took as it froze her chest and stabbed her lungs like a knife. She crashed to her knees and the impact wouldn't have been different if a bolt of lightning had run through her body. How could she have gotten here? It was a good hour's walk from what she remembered, she couldn't have come all this way without knowing it.

At first, she thought she was dreaming but the pain she felt was too sharp for her to make up. She wouldn't have been able to inflict such pain on herself through her dreams. She looked around her, it was dark but the sky was clear and the moon was almost full. The light was diffuse and misty, it all felt so real, she even held the snow in the palm of her hands, numbed out by the icy cold. Her fingers were almost blue, and she had trouble bending them. She stared out to the place she had seen the woman hours before. It was empty. The moonlight made the snow on the ground look like velvet.

A rustle caught her ears, and she looked to the direction from which it came. She couldn't believe her eyes, there it was, beautiful and almost magical, and it slowly walked towards her. Even if she could move she would have been afraid it would have run away as it had before. As he approached her, his antlers seemed gigantic, she reached out to them and was surprised by the velvety feel of them. They both looked into each other's eyes for a while and then the elk ran off to where he had come from. She watched him run till her eyes could no longer discern him. He disappeared into the darkness and the sound of his hoofs died out into the snowy hills.

"You do have a gift," a voice whispered out.

She turned to search all around her to see where the words had come from. She saw nothing.

"You must be aware of it and use it," the voice continued.

"Who is there?" she tried to cry out but her voice was the faintest sound she'd made, her heart pounding so hard and fast she thought it was going to burst out of her chest.

"Be not afraid, I mean no harm. Quite the contrary."

"Why can't I see you?"

"You do not need to see, you know who I am now."

"Why me? Why not Samuel or Taylor?"

"Because you can hear and you can see. They can't and I don't want them to."

"Why not?"

"You'll understand soon enough."

Those were the last words Estelle heard as her body was giving up on her, she couldn't resist anymore, she let go, and she slipped as if she were falling into a huge dark hole, and then she violently hit the ground. Silence and darkness.

| 14 |

Blessed was the day Estelle ran away from Seattle, from Dan, or whatever she was running away from. If she hadn't all this wouldn't have happened. She would still be in her apartment staring at her computer trying to come up with something new and, of course, she wouldn't have met Taylor and Samuel, of whom she was now very fond. She started to wonder how long she could pull this off. How much time did she have until Dan decided to come and bring her back to Seattle? Besides, Taylor was on vacation, and he would soon have to go back to work. What about Samuel? She knew he wouldn't let her go easily after the conversation they had had the other night. He was convinced the woman she kept seeing was his deceased sister. She then remembered one of his questions that had puzzled her.

"What were you thinking of before the crash?" was what he had asked her.

The words rang back and forth inside her ears. A question

she had thought so strange she had disregarded it but now, in the light of the recent events, she wondered how he could have known. She suddenly remembered the flash she had had yesterday at the sight of the crash. The other car and that woman, that woman who was crossing the road unafraid in the frosty darkness, that woman the car was trying to avoid. It couldn't be! Was that woman who, in her flash, had provoked the crash, the same woman she had been seeing all this time? If so, why and why Estelle?

She kept running the scene inside her head, over and over again in slow motion. Was it really what had happened or was it just her imagination? All she could focus on was the woman who seemed to be walking effortlessly with her long black hair waving behind her and her complexion had a sort of glow or fluorescence like a faint neon light fluttering through the snowflakes. An acute and creaky sound interrupted her brain and the worst migraine she had ever experienced paralyzed her thoughts as tiny white shiny dots stained her vision. Her body stiffened up and her breathing died out becoming difficult and painful when a violent sting ran through her entire body from head to toe.

Blank. In the silence of the night, she lay in bed wrestling motionless and almost breathless. No one was there to pull her out of the strain this time. Her hands clenched to the pillow underneath her head, sweat oozing out of her every pore, her eyes wide open transfixed to the ceiling, and her mouth open.

Samuel was torn from his sleep, something drew him to the room Estelle was sleeping in. He came in without the slightest sound and saw Estelle mildly convulsing in bed. He carefully approached her and touched her cheek then placed both of his hands, palms down, over her heart, murmuring a chant as he fell into some sort of trance. Eventually, Estelle stopped convulsing after a violent shake and lay perfectly still. The lines of her face had relaxed, and she seemed appeased. At one point, her hands reached out to Samuel's arms, his hands still gently pressuring her heart, and muttered inaudible words. Samuel was still concentrated and at last Estelle's body entirely loosened followed by a long and heavy sigh. The room gained a few degrees in seconds and Samuel stopped his incantation, wiped her face, placed another blanket over her, and left the room.

The intervention had exhausted him. He crashed onto the couch, where he had fallen asleep the night before. After Dan's call, Estelle had gone off to bed to be alone while Samuel and Taylor stayed together near the fireplace, talking about what they had done in the last three years. Taylor confessed he had done nothing but survive and felt he was changing since Estelle showed up. He became a patrol officer because Allister put him to it to take his mind off things. Taylor admitted he had sunk into the routine and become addicted to it.

Samuel remained silent most of the time and analyzed Taylor's words and reactions. He knew something had died inside him when Koko's death had been announced. Taylor and Koko had been inseparable since the day they met. They spent practically every second together. This had even annoyed the people at the reservation. They liked Taylor but they were afraid the relationship would tear Koko away from her goals but she never let anything get in the way of that, and those who knew her well, knew that.

| 15 |

When dawn broke into Estelle's room she felt exhausted. She tried to go back to sleep but it was no use. She tossed and turned for some time and finally gave up. She looked through the window and still couldn't believe how beautiful the place was. It was as if she had been drawn to this place by some invisible force. She didn't know where it was on a map nor if it were anywhere near where she had decided on going when she had left Seattle. She despised reading maps and put too much faith in her GPS, so she hadn't even bothered checking the route before leaving. She was surprised she hadn't felt the urge of using the internet yet. She had to admit she had become an addict, compulsively checking her emails and Googling anything that crossed her mind.

When she left Seattle, she was heading for Yellowstone, a place she had always dreamt of going to. She had never traveled on her own like that. Normally, the thought of doing something alone would have stressed her out for days. She did not know what had triggered the impulse. Was it simply the anger or the deception? Or was she just waiting for a good excuse to trick and comfort her conscience into change? Whatever it was, there she was in the middle of someplace she hadn't planned on being, and she wasn't the least anguished about it. Things had not been easy on her, even though she could not complain, she had a rather normal life and upbringing, she did have some emotional scars here and there. Some hard to express and deal with.

From start to finish she felt her entire life had been a disaster. Her parents were still together, but she had no clue why. They couldn't stand each other, her mother had taken up a passion for alcohol and parties and her father spent his time in a bubble. They never even talked to each other and when they did they argued. She despised having to see them. Every time she did, because she felt guilty she wasn't involved enough in their life, she just sat there wishing she had never come. Her guilty conscious always had the last word, and she hated it. She was very calm but felt that in those particular moments she could be violent and possessed by anger. So she remained quiet and made up an excuse to leave.

Now that she was in America, thousands of miles away, that feeling had disappeared. She felt no obligation towards them whatsoever. She hardly ever called them and it was the same on their side, except on some occasions when her mother would call her up completely drunk and she would start repeating the same old things over and over and over again. This made Estelle want to break the phone line, rip it out of the wall and throw the receiver so it would smash against something and break into a million tiny pieces, but instead of letting her instinct burst out she took everything in and patiently waited for the right moment to say goodbye and then she would sit there looking at the phone trying to find solutions but there were none and a new day would come and sweep away her preoccupations until the next time. It was hard for her not to feel responsible for her parents as an adult and see how unhappy they were. Even though she knew it wasn't her role to act like a parent for her parents she relentlessly tried to help them. But nothing changed, it just hurt her more and more.

The virgin white landscape appeased her, there in the silence of the dawn. The room was empty but filled with a warm feeling. She could stand there for hours and not feel like she had to occupy herself. A gentle knock on the door pulled Estelle out of her reveries. The knob turned gently, and she could make out the outlines of Samuel's face. Estelle drew a confused smile at the sight of him.

"Just checking up on you, how are you feeling?" Samuel said whispering.

"Just fine Samuel, thanks," she replied curiously eyeing him.

"No bad dreams or visions?" he asked half-mockingly.

She shook her head and smiled. She could feel herself start to blush and it made her uncomfortable. She put her head down so that her hair would cover her face but Samuel's silent stare didn't help. The time he stood there looking at her felt like an eternity.

"Hey, guys ready for breakfast?" Taylor's light voice ripped the heavy silence. "Am I interrupting something?" his tone changing when he noticed their faces.

"No, I was just checking up on Estelle, you know, if her night was vision-free if you see what I mean. And it's all good," Samuel said tapping Taylor's shoulder. "Let's get some breakfast, I could eat a wolf!" his voice fainted as it disappeared in the distance of the hallway.

Taylor stood in the doorway, looking at Estelle, still head down, dying to take her in his arms but some unknown force kept him at a safe distance from her. Feeling his presence Estelle lifted her head in his direction and felt uncomfortable, almost sick. All the lightness she had felt just minutes before had vanished and turned to oppression. They both stood there speechless and motionless like blocked pawns on a chessboard, no matter the move someone will die.

For both Taylor and Estelle, that specific moment in their lives did feel like a game of chess, the next move would profoundly change their lives. Their hesitation danced around them and played with them. Something had to break or something had to give.

"It's a good sign that you've had a good night's sleep, it means you're getting better," Taylor's fatherly voice broke the awkward silence at last.

"Yeah, it's a relief," she said without meaning it. For her, getting better was synonymous with returning to Seattle, and she couldn't picture herself doing that. "Did you ever get the impression something important happened in your dream but you can't remember a thing? A total blackout," she bounced back to him, scrutinizing his reaction.

"Sure, it happens sometimes, that's normal," he answered not the least bit worried.

This annoyed her, she wanted him to worry about her, she felt that the more normal things would get the more un-attentive Taylor and Samuel would become, and the more her old life would come running back to her. Back to Dan, back to her parents, and reality. Reality. She hated that word and everything it reflected. Everything was so unreal since the accident, so perfect and unpredictable. She didn't want this movie to end, not in the middle of things. She felt something was slipping away, and she was determined to get it back and hold on to it tightly, she had to get back on the dream.

In vain, Estelle waited for a vision. She desperately wanted Koko or whoever the woman was to come back. She had become the fuel of the whole situation. Now the reservoir was running dry and the engine was starting to weaken. The day was more than halfway through and nothing unexpected or expected had happened. All three had stayed around the house, not doing much without even talking. As if the game were on pause. Estelle couldn't focus her attention on anything, she couldn't keep a straight conversation and could not watch the programs on television or follow what Samuel and Taylor were talking about.

The house that had at first seemed gigantic to her now felt constricted and confined. Her heart felt oppressed and heavy. She thought each beat would burst it open, and then they would care, then they would pay attention to how she felt. Deep inside she couldn't stand herself, she did not understand why she was thriving this much for attention from two perfect strangers, two beautiful strangers, each different in their way. She hated that she had to fall into attraction with almost every man she met and fall right out of it once she had gotten full reward for it. She knew it was coming, and she did not want that, she was struggling to avoid this. Dan was enough to handle at this point.

She stared at Taylor's face whenever she could without being noticed, trying to engrave his every feature in her mind. She did not know what made him so attractive, his electric green-blueish eyes or his strongly persuasive smile. Not that she had seen him smile much but had managed to catch it in a flash as it appeared and disappeared but remained lingering in his eyes. Or was it his overall calmness and false detachment that drew her to him? She could not explain. Samuel was very different, but also very intense. He was undefinable, unreadable. Something fierce and wild, something that could not be tamed, could not be gamed. If he were an element he would certainly be fire. He made her feel uncomfortable as if he could read inside her and it frightened her, she was afraid of his judgment.

"Estelle, Estelle? Hello?" Taylor's voice broke through her thoughts.

"We're going into town, you can come with us if you're up to it or stay here," he said gently.

"Sure, are you leaving right away, or do I have time to get ready?"

"Go ahead, we'll wait, it'll do you good to see a change of décor," he said with a smile.

Estelle smiled back avoiding his eyes then she jumped up

and headed to her room swiftly. She was excited. She got ready as fast as she could and arrived just in time to get into the car. They had been clearing the snow that had piled up over it. The engine roared and echoed as an uninvited guest in the middle of this lush nature-filled landscape. The seat was frozen and Estelle was boiling inside from the excitement of the unexpected she had learned to love.

The white branches brushed by as tears filled her eyes, eyes she could not close unwilling to let anything pass her by. She wanted as much as she could get as if everything could disappear in a blink. She could see Taylor was used to driving through these steep snowy roads, and she wondered how she had gotten so far that night. She had never driven in such weather, had she known she would never even have taken the road. She would have stopped at a hotel to wait it out. She trusted Taylor but still could not look out the window when there was a precipice as if just looking down could make them fall. But the view was breathtaking, so she gazed far off avoiding the precipice.

"Everything okay back there?" Samuel s voice rang from the front seat.

"Yes, admiring the view," Estelle replied her eyes glued to the window.

"We're almost there," Taylor said in a strong voice trying to cover the engine and the music.

Estelle was surprised, she hadn't seen the hour pass being so absorbed by the scenery. Soon the view of the mountains disappeared to give way to bunches of pine trees and houses and then a big avenue of stores and restaurants. Estelle loved it but couldn't remember passing it before. The street was empty except for a few men shoveling snow from the door-ways and driveways. Not much looked open.

Taylor turned off the main street and parked in front of a store. Both men got out of the car and before Estelle could move an inch Taylor had already opened her door to help her down. Once out of the car she could make out the name of the store: Polly's Country Foods. She followed Taylor inside and was surprised by the heat inside.

" Look what the tide brought in," cried out a warm voice from behind the counter. "I thought I wasn't going to see you around here till next week," she continued inspecting Estelle from head to toe as they walked towards her. Her smile could not be any wider until her eyes landed on Samuel and a cross look came upon her face. Her eyes bounced back to Taylor puzzled and confused. "Well, I must be getting old for sur-prises," she finally managed to say to cool things down. She avoided Samuel's glare and found refuge in examining Estelle again. "I don't believe we've met, have we?" the warmness in her voice had reappeared.

"No, Mam, this here is Estelle. I believe the Doc must have told you about her," Taylor said as if everything were normal.

"Oh, my goodness, yes! I didn't think she would be up and about so quickly from what he told me. I see you've been a good care-taker," she exclaimed rubbing the palms of her hands together as to warm them up.

"Samuel has been a lot of help in Estelle's recovery," Tay-lor added proudly.

"Oh, good, I'm very happy. This is great news. And like I said, this is drastic weather and anything could happen once caught off guard for a fraction of a second. "Polly's eyes traveled back onto Samuel and a timid smile started to be drawn on her lips and was completely erased by Samuel's cold and piercing eyes. "How you've grown into a fine young man," the words escaped her before she could hold them back and Estelle could have sworn tears had started to fill her eyes but nothing ran down her cheek. Invisible tears. "So what can I do for you young people today?"

"Well, I didn't expect having two permanent guests over the last time I came," Taylor said in a light and joyful tone.

"Go ahead and suit yourself, I've had no deliveries so might not find all you need. No trucks are coming up, not before next week."

Estelle wandered around the aisles, the store was cute and fairly big. She liked the wooden logs all over the walls and ceiling and the smell of it. She had lost sight of Taylor and Samuel. She gazed at all the little souvenirs, little carved statues of bears and wolves, dreamcatchers, hand-made jewelry, and books on Glacier National Park and Native American tribes. All of a sudden she could smell fresh hot coffee coming from the back of the store, not far from where she was. She was looking through the pictures of a book about the Blackfeet Indians. She was looking for a face that looked like her visions when the weight of a hand on her shoulder startled her.

"Sorry, I didn't mean to frighten you," said a familiar voice.

Estelle raised her eyes following the hand and recognized the Doctor's face. He was tall, she hadn't noticed that before.

"You look a lot better compared to the last time I saw you," he continued. "I'm glad," he added smiling. "So you're out sight-seeing in this wonderful weather?" he said joking.

"I guess," Estelle answered quite shy and blushing.

"So you into Indians are you?" he asked looking at the book she had in her hands.

"Just looking through it," she said shrugging her shoulders as she felt his grip harden on her shoulder. She looked at his face to see he was focused on Samuel's face.

"Estelle, we're finished here. We're leaving," Samuel said coldly without looking at her. Henry released his grip still staring at Samuel. Estelle put the book back down and headed towards the exit where Taylor was waiting. She hurried her pace to warn him that Samuel and Henry were in back but before she reached him Samuel was by her side. Taylor thanked Polly and opened the door for Estelle. All three entered the car silently and the engine roared seconds after.

Not a soul could be seen in the street. The sun was on its way down and the sky was half white half orange. The silence had not left the car. It was still there as heavy as ever. Estelle was starting to get quite acquainted with this brand-new companion. It wasn't disturbing but it was palpable as if it entered and left places just like a person. None of them tried to intrude and break it. When it finally decided to leave the atmosphere became lighter and Taylor turned on the radio volume quite low, she could feel he was extra concentrated on the road. It was dark as they pulled into the driveway.

All three relaxed as they got out of the car. Samuel and Taylor got the groceries out of the trunk. On the way to the house, Taylor looked at Shakespeare and said, " I know boy, I've been no good these past few days. I'll make it up to you. Don't worry." The horse seemed to nod at him in agreement and went back into the warmth of the shed. As

Samuel approached the door he stiffened and turned to look at Taylor and raising his hand with a sign not to walk any closer. Samuel cautiously opened the door and ventured into the dark house.

Taylor could not look away from the door. He hesitated a while before he put the bags he was carrying down on the porch. He made a sign to Estelle to stay where she was. He entered the house as well. Estelle was beginning to feel insecure alone in the dark. Her head started to spin a little, and she leaned on the car to rest. When she raised her head in direction of the house to see if any light had been turned on she saw nothing. The house had disappeared. Estelle closed her eyes and breathed in and out slowly. She then opened her eyes again and still nothing. She wasn't leaning on Taylor's car anymore but on a rock, a huge rock. The shed was gone as well. Before her eyes could focus on the surroundings she saw a faint light moving swiftly towards her. Her heart was pounding, afraid of what she would see next.

Instead of seeing anything, she heard a whisper from behind. A frozen breeze ran down her neck.

"This is how it was before they came here. This was ours. All of it," said the murmured voice into her ear.

"When who came?" Estelle asked wondering if it spoke of Taylor.

"You know who. Who is THEY in this town? Can't you feel who the WE are? Don't you naturally feel closer to some than to others?"

"What about the house?" Estelle asked trying to understand.

"Nothing, I have a feeling someone visited it while we

were out, you feeling alright?" Samuel's voice crushed in completely unexpected. The puzzled look on her face did not need further explanations for Samuel. He knew. He bent down and lifted her and carried her inside. She kept looking at the house in awe. The moment Samuel's foot stepped into the house, Estelle could feel it, deep inside. She could feel someone other than them had been inside. Something she could not describe. She stared into Samuel's eyes and told him to put her down. She walked directly to her room and knew someone had gone through her things. Samuel was right behind her.

"They went through my things," she cried out frantically obsessively running her hands through her hair. "Why the hell would someone go through my things? What is this place?" she yelled out at Samuel.

"Estelle, calm down. I know someone was here. Why I can't say. But let's not panic Taylor with this. Okay, can we keep this between us, please, Estelle?" he said holding her hands away from her hair then wiped her angry tears. "There's nothing to be afraid of, I promise. Trust me," he continued now holding her in his arms in a tight embrace, so tight she had to free her face to be able to breathe. He was as hard as stone; she would never be able to break the embrace if he hadn't decided to release her. He did not seem that strong when you looked at him. Estelle was surprised and decided to listen to him, and she promised she would not mention the subject to Taylor.

"I don't know who was here, but it was a very clean job," Estelle muttered as she tried to free herself from the embrace.

She stumbled when he let go as Taylor's voice cried out from the kitchen:

"Hey Sam, when you're finished chasing whatever you are chasing could you get some logs for the fireplace? It's getting pretty chilly in here."

Samuel's eyes requested one last silent promise from Estelle before he left the room. Had not the end of the day been on such an awkward note Estelle would have probably enjoyed a bath before dinner. But Polly and Henry's strange reactions, the heavy silence on the way back, the voice, the house, and now this feeling of being spied on was more than enough for her to not want to stay alone. She joined Taylor in the kitchen as soon as she had changed into comfortable clothes for the evening.

| 17 |

"Did you find anything interesting?" said the voice on the other end of the line.

"Not much, a bunch of junk love letters and tons of poetry or something like that but nothing else."

"Damn it... I'm sure she's hiding something. You don't just get here by accident as she did!"

"Yeah, and the way she has that damn Indian boy following her around all the time doesn't make sense, we better keep an eye on him."

"Taylor I can handle, but Samuel, is going to be very difficult."

| 18 |

Estelle never liked conflict, and she could sense it when something was about to hit, and she felt it. Something important. She cautiously avoided Taylor's eyes throughout that evening. She didn't understand why he was the only one to not have felt that someone had come into the house while they were away. Something linked her to Samuel, but she could not put her finger on it. She kept thinking of him, his questions, his looks, and his intrusions. She did not feel uncomfortable in his presence, but he did create an undefinable feeling when he was near. She was now more drawn to him than to Taylor because he intrigued her. He enclosed much more mystery and layer than Taylor did.

Estelle's emerald eyes had been staring into the fire for so long she had not even noticed they were crying until Taylor wiped her cheeks and kneeled as to gaze into her eyes directly. She tried not to look at him but was unable to resist. She tried not to make him feel her recent attempts to distance him. But Taylor caught more subtle things than he let on.

"I wish I could do more right now, I wish I could explain what is going on here," he said squeezing her hands in his.

Estelle was speechless, had she been wrong about Taylor? Why hadn't he expressed this before? She remained cautious in her words.

"What would you want to explain?" she asked in a broken eerie voice.

"You know what I mean Estelle. Polly and Henry's strange behavior, the Sheriff too. There's just something that doesn't seem to fit the picture. Even Samuel, I try to not pay attention to his theories and despising reactions such as at the store earlier on. I just don't know why he keeps hating them so much, after all these years. He should let go. I really don't even understand why he's back."

When Estelle lifted her head to look Taylor in the eyes she saw the woman at his place, holding her hands as he was. Estelle could not move. She stared the woman in the eyes.

"Do not speak, just listen," said the woman.

"I am not here to hurt you nor Taylor. Taylor is lost at the moment, but he will find his way through this. Things will slowly come back to him, and he will understand. Samuel is here to guide you. You must help him find me. You are the only way the truth can be discovered. I have already used up a lot of energy to get through to you and will weaken as time goes by. Make out the pieces I give to you."

"And I don't even know how I can make things easier, are you listening to me?" Taylor's voice returned as the woman vanished.

Estelle shivered and hugged Taylor to divert him, she had not followed a word he had been saying, and she whispered, "I'm exhausted," in his ear. She predicted he would carry her to bed without saying one more thing, and he did. What she hadn't predicted was that he would stay with her. He lay down next to her and turned the light out. She fell asleep in his arms relieved he was there. She did not want to stay alone that night. Not after someone had been through her things.

| 19 |

That morning all three were pulled out of bed by an insistent ringing of the doorbell. Taylor rubbed his eyes, looked at Estelle somewhat confused, wondering who would be ringing his doorbell like that. He was slow to get out of bed and by the time he reached the living-room, Samuel had already opened the door and was talking to a man Taylor had never seen before. It didn't take him long before he made out the man was no one else but Dan. Taylor's heart stopped beating for several seconds and then started pacing like crazy. He took a deep breath to slow it down. He didn't even know Dan but deeply hated him.

"You must be Taylor?" Dan said as he walked towards him confidently his arm reaching out for a handshake and an ultra-bright smiled sewed onto his face.

Taylor snapped out of his inner torment and accepted the handshake mechanically, fixing Dan in the eyes as if in a duel.

Both men met in an electric exchange and Samuel could feel the tension in both of them fill up the room.

"We weren't expecting you so soon," Taylor finally let out.

Dan was about to reply but remained speechless as his eyes caught sight of Estelle coming into the room.

"Estelle," he said pacing towards her. He grabbed her in such a tight embrace she thought he had crushed her ribs in.

"I was so worried about you, you nearly killed me with worry," he said in a low voice so that only she could hear. " I'm so sorry, please forgive me," he added.

Estelle remained silent and still for a while. Those few minutes felt endless and painful to Taylor who had been doing nothing else than standing there staring at them. Samuel attempted to break the picture by saying:

"Let's all have a seat in the kitchen and enjoy a cup of coffee together. I'm going to make some now."

"Great idea, I'll prepare some toast as well," Taylor said eager to leave the room and fill his eyes with a different view.

Dan finally released Estelle from his embrace. They both looked at each other in the eyes observingly.

"I can't believe you drove all this way to see me," Estelle broke out.

"I didn't just come to see you, I came to bring you back to Seattle," he replied hardly holding his excitement in.

Estelle suddenly pushed him away and said in a dry and cold voice Dan remembered but too well:

"What makes you think I want to go back? I never asked you to come here, did I?" Dan was hurt but not completely surprised although he had hoped she would not react that way and that the accident would have made her feel differently towards him. He now knew he had been wrong.

"Estelle, you are aware that you have a contract to honor and that we can't put our work off much longer. I'm aware that you just had a terrible accident and that it isn't making anything easier on you and I'm sorry. I truly want to help, but I need you to be willing to accept my help. For the moment Spencer is being pretty nice about all this, but he will start hassling me soon about the project. We do have a deadline. I need him to at least think we are working and that would be a lot easier if you were in Seattle with me. He is not going to pay for your apartment and work VISA forever, and we need him to support you or else it's over. I'm sorry to be harsh but it's the truth and even if it's a hard moment you have to face it. Let me help you, please Estelle. Don't ruin everything now."

Estelle stood there speechless as her brain tried to analyze everything he had just said. Reality had just splashed into her face.

"Come now let's go sit down with your friends and have some coffee while you think things over calmly," he said in a caring tone as he led her towards where he had seen both men go.

Estelle dragged herself along absorbed in her thoughts as she sat down without making eye contact with anyone. She drifted away in inner questions and lists as they all started a casual conversation about Montana and its weather. Their words fluttered around her like leaves in a storm. She felt isolated and unable to make a decision afraid to regret whichever path she would choose to take. Both meaning the loss of something she was deeply attached to. Deep down she knew she had to go back to Seattle. It might as well be the sooner the better before she became too attached to leave.

Estelle's voice interrupted their conversation about how cold it was in winter.

"I'm going back to Seattle with Dan; I have to pack my things."

Taylor's jaw cracked as he tried to hide the sudden burst of emotion that filled his chest. His arms felt numb so did his feet. He could not move his lips or say a thing when Samuel's voice scorched out like fire.

"What! Now? You can't leave now!"

"I'm sorry Sam but I have to go, I have work to get done and it doesn't just depend on me. I'm truly sorry, please bear with me," she said.

Dan was surprised by their outspoken intimacy and reactions towards each other as if something held them together like brothers and sisters. The atmosphere confused him, and he started to feel very uncomfortable and unwanted. He felt an indescribable heaviness come upon him and his breathing started to feel difficult. He started sweating and his mouth was feeling dry, he swallowed more coffee to make the dryness disappear but his mouth became drier and drier. He decided to get out of the room and get some air.

"Excuse me I need to make a phone call," he said getting up from his chair.

No one answered or even paid attention to him as he left the room. All three sat there waiting for someone to talk. Samuel came next to Estelle and said:

"You can't leave."

"Stop saying that Samuel! Why can't she leave? What binds her here? Nothing! So stop saying that!" Taylor said coldly and annoyed.

"Estelle, we completely understand that you have to go even if we enjoy your company and will miss you. But you have to do what you have to do, we just didn't think it would be so soon and abrupt," he managed to say in a detached tone he hated himself for.

Estelle could not find the words that would feel right, and she preferred to hug him, she knew he was hurt and did not want to make anything worse. As for Samuel, she felt like a traitor. She could only say she was sorry once more and left the room to pack her things.

She passed Dan on her way into her room without looking at him. He was sitting on the couch next to the fireplace wondering what could have happened between the three of them. He was intrigued but was somewhat afraid to know. His main and only concern was to bring Estelle back to Seattle. To get her back to work, to convince Spencer everything was fine and that the work was being done. He was just put off by the strange atmosphere he had just entered. He expected Estelle's reaction would not be the most welcoming, but he did not expect such an awkward ambiance. He felt like he was interrupting or intruding. The strangest scenarios played through his head as he waited for Estelle to pack.

| 20 |

Estelle walked into her room trying to breathe every single detail in. She suddenly felt an acute pain in her chest and sat on the bed waiting for it to go away. As she sat there she stared at her reflection in the mirror across from her. She knew something had changed not only inside her but also on the outside. Her face was more serious and marked than it had been before. She ran her fingers down her cheek and through her hair but could not figure out what had changed, but she felt different. Her hands started to shake at first she could hardly notice and little by little she could not control them anymore, they shook so hard that her fingers were numb and her wrists were aching. And the shaking suddenly stopped.

"You are letting us down! I was wrong to trust you with this," the woman's now familiar voice said.

Estelle looked all around the room to see her but could not find her.

"Don't bother, you won't be able to see me, my powers have already started to faint I can now only use my voice, and soon that too will disappear. We have little time left. Too little." This time her voice was cold and eerie.

"I can't stay here any longer and I don't know how I can help, I want to help but I really don't know what I'm supposed to do. How am I supposed to help Samuel find you?" Estelle replied in a desperate voice.

"I told you, you are the only one. Samuel can feel things but since I am too close to him, he is my brother, I cannot connect with him. It is the same for Taylor; I can only connect to their dreams."

"Why is it you connect with me?" Estelle asked confused.

"I don't know, I have tried to connect with someone for years and never could, I can't explain this either. There is hardly anyone new passing by these roads, and I am stuck here. I have been stuck here since the accident. Well, not exactly an accident. Everything had been planned, the crash was not an accident but cold-blooded murder and I have to make the truth come out."

"An accident? That's what Samuel's feeling was, that it wasn't an accident. Do you mean someone wanted to kill you and disguised it into an accident? That is horrible! Who is it?" Estelle asked in shock.

"Not just one person organized this, and they will all stick together. They think they are safe behind their titles but inside they are eaten by guilt."

"But who are they?"

"Who are they?" Estelle repeated the question but there was no answer but a knock at her door.

Taylor opened the door slowly making sure he wasn't intruding.

"Can I come in?" he asked still behind the door.

"Sure," she said trying to look as if nothing special had been going on.

"So, this is it. You're leaving. I'm sorry I am not as expressive as I should or even want to be."

"Don't worry, I feel you, and believe me this isn't what I want to do but I have to. I wish I could stay here longer. I wish this wasn't so sudden."

"Well, you did get here out of the blue so you might as well leave that way too. All I want to say is, this is not easy for me, sorry. I'd like for us to keep in touch, well, if you agree. If not it's fine, no hard feelings," he said unable to look her in the eyes as he expressed those words.

"Of course, of course, we'll stay in touch," she said putting her hand on his and squeezing it.

Taylor felt a weight lift off of him and could breathe normally again.

"Maybe I'll have to come out to Seattle sometime for a visit, never been there so might as well plan a trip soon."

Estelle smiled, and he started helping her pack her things and brought everything to the door ready to go.

Estelle asked Samuel to come and talk to her in private. A very angry Samuel followed her into the room. He waited for her to start talking as he stood near the door.

"Samuel, please don't be angry with me. I am not letting you down, nor Koko nor Taylor."

"You're leaving, I don't see how things could get better," he hit back.

"My visions are becoming rare and Koko told me she was getting weak, that she could not continue connecting with me. I can't see her any longer, I can only hear her now. She said something about the accident not being an accident but intentional. She said that people had planned the accident. It was murder Samuel, murder."

"When, when did she say that?"

"Just a few minutes ago, before Taylor came to help me pack."

"Who was it? Who killed them?" Samuel asked impatiently.

"What do you mean by them?" Estelle asked confused.

"Well, Koko did not die alone in that accident, she was with Taylor's parents that day driving to the lake," Samuel said.

"Oh, I'm sorry I didn't know. She didn't say who it was she just said it was several people that planned it and that they will stick together and something about hiding behind their titles but inside they feel guilty."

Samuel listened, trying to make out these words as Estelle was putting her purse over her shoulder. She walked towards him and said nothing. She just stared into his fiery eyes and put her hand around his wrist, flexed her toes to win a few inches and kissed his cheek softly then walked out of the room.

Samuel stood there not wanting to see her leave, so he waited there until he heard the engine roar, the tires back out of the driveway, and Taylor close the door. Samuel's knuckles turned blue from the tight fist he had been holding them into since she left the room. With Estelle leaving the hope of Koko finding peace had disappeared. What had led him back here after so long? He knew he could not help Koko but her last words to Estelle confirmed the feeling he had nurtured since her death.

| 21 |

Estelle sat in the front seat next to Dan watching the house move away with a strong pinching in her heart. She wanted to hold her arms out and grab it back to her and take it along with her. Tears ran down her face onto her shiny red purse as the house disappeared and was but a translucent stain in her eyes. She swallowed her tears so that Dan didn't notice her crying.

Dan drove very slowly, he wasn't used to driving on steep snowy roads and Estelle could sense how hard it must have been on his nerves to drive up all the way to Taylor's. He wouldn't take his eyes off the road afraid he would miss a turn. He did not have Taylor's confidence and Estelle could not relax completely as she sunk into the passenger's seat. Hence, Estelle didn't even attempt to break the silence had she had anything to say.

She watched the flittering white landscape as she had the day before. This time with sadness. She always had a strange feeling when she passed the place where her car had crashed. Of course, it wasn't there anymore, but she could see the trees the car had damaged as they passed that turn. The vision of Koko walking on that snowy road that night was ever so clear in her memory now. She reached out slowly, not to alarm Dan, and raised the heater's temperature, she was freezing cold.

They had already passed Polly's Country Foods when she saw Koko's wavering apparition in front of the store. As she turned to look from the rear-view window Koko had vanished. It was at that moment that Estelle was struck by an intense panic, she had not thought of noting Taylor's number, how would she contact him. Her pulse started to race and tears started running down her cheeks uncontrolled.

"How can I be so stupid?" she said out loud without realizing.

"Why do you say that?" Dan asked having relaxed a little.

She looked at him puzzled: "I don't have their number."

Dan laughed out loud and shook his head. "Estelle, I have it, remember I called you and I came all the way up there so relax," he answered with a friendly pat on her knee.

Estelle couldn't believe how strange her brain had been acting since the accident. All the little insignificant things she felt she couldn't process anymore. Her heart grew heavier the further they drove away from Blackmont. The sun had disappeared behind thick snow-filled clouds as they continued their smooth drive towards Seattle. Dan turned the radio on but found nothing. He kept flipping from station to station and turned it off, lit a cigarette instead. Dan had a lot of trouble doing nothing.

He inhaled the first puff deeply and blocked the smoke in for a few seconds and slowly expired the smoke out. Estelle realized she hadn't missed smoking. She accepted the cigarette he offered her and the nicotine soothed her nerves for a moment. A few hours after having left Taylor's, Dan pulled up at a gas station to fill the tank. They both went inside and had some coffee. She could see that Dan was fighting to hide the fact that he was tired.

"We can stop somewhere if you want to rest you know," she slipped in between two sips of coffee.

Dan didn't answer he was too busy looking at the lady behind the counter eyeing Estelle. He knew she stood out in her style and it just bugged him to see how people were narrow-minded enough to think she wasn't just a normal person.

"Dan?" she insisted.

"Oh, no, Estelle, I'm fine, might as well push it to Seattle," he mechanically answered still deep in his thoughts.

He finally snapped out of it and got up abruptly, took her empty paper cup to pile it into his. She followed him as he walked towards the exit and threw both cups in the trash on the way out. The door rang as they opened it and passed through it. The cold hit them hard, and they paced to the car. He started the car and a few hours later they could catch a glimpse of the city lights in the distance. The lights gave the impression of watercolors through the rainy windshield. Dan was now driving his regular 100 miles an hour. The night had fallen a while ago, and she kept an eye on him. He had been driving all day and the car would go out of its lane here and there.

Dan parked into Estelle's garage. He turned the engine off and got out of the car to open the trunk.

"Go upstairs, I'll bring your things up," he yelled out from behind the car.

She slowly went up the dark staircase that led to her living-room. It felt strange to be back, but she didn't feel as bad as she thought she would. She turned the lights on so that Dan wouldn't have trouble coming up with all her things and saw he had set the table and a bottle of wine, Pinot Noir, as usual, his favorite, and he knew she enjoyed it too. There was a note next to the wine and a bouquet and fresh flowers. She bent over to reach it and opened it carefully not to rip anything. It simply read:

"I'm sorry, I will never do this again, I feel silly, please forgive me."

She put the note back inside the envelope and set it back where he had put it as she heard his steps reach the living-room. He continued another flight of stairs to put her suitcase in her bedroom and then came back down with a tired and worn-out face.

"Ok, Estelle, I'm heading home but if you don't want to be alone I can stay," he tried to say in a very casual way afraid she might interpret it in a wrong way but she didn't. She was very calm and said with a warm smile:

"I'll be fine Dan, thank you for the offer. I'm exhausted and I'm going to go to bed."

He was relieved and gave her a goodbye hug and left.

She waited to hear his car pull out of her garage, and she buzzed the garage door close. She stood there in the middle of her living-room and felt peaceful. Maybe she was too tired to feel sad. She turned the electric fireplace on, turned the dim lamps on instead of the aggressive ceiling lights. She opened the bottle of wine and poured herself a glass. On her way back into the living-room she took a cigarette from one of the drawers and comfortably sat on the couch in front of the artificial fire. She stared into it as she drank and smoked.

Her thoughts were empty for once, and she sat there savoring the moment when the ringing of her BlackBerry startled her. She tried to make out where the sound came from as she didn't know where Dan had put her purse. She hadn't heard it ring for so long that it felt pretty aggressive. She hurried to find it to stop the annoying ringing sound going through her head. She finally found it and saw her mother's phone number. She wasn't in the mood to talk to her, so she muted her phone. When she came back to the home page she saw all the missed calls, text messages, voicemail, and emails that had appeared. She put the phone on the table and returned to the couch.

The sudden outburst of technology reminded her she was back. Back to reality. She wanted to remain disconnected from the virtual life one more night. She would deal with it soon enough. She watched the fake flames dance around in a completely unnatural way till they all became a huge sparkling orange circle. Sleep had taken over for the night in the more than calm city winter. The sound of cars passing by filled the room every few minutes as the sound of a plane would complete the orchestra of the city's symphony.

| **22** |

"She's gone. She left the house this morning. It's just Samuel now," said the voice on the other side of the receiver.

"Samuel's not the easiest one to get rid of, I really wonder what made him come back after all this time. There must be something going on," the second voice answered worryingly.

"Do you honestly believe he found something out, it's impossible? There's absolutely no way."

"I don't know, they have their ways."

"Bullshit, you believe in those spiritual things now, you of all people."

"I'm just saying it's beyond our understanding sometimes. I come to doubt with age."

"You're just afraid because you're getting old, there's nothing tangible in your reasoning."

The other voice remained silent.

"Ok, I'll leave you to your new thoughts, in the meantime I'll keep an eye on Sam. I'll let you know if there's anything strange going on. Taylor should be back soon since the girl's gone."

"Alright.", said the other voice and they both hung up.

| **23** |

Samuel had been silent and kept to himself since Estelle had left. Rummaging through his memories and Estelle's words before she took off.

Taylor, on the other hand, had been out most of the time, taking care of Shakespeare and working around the house in general. They both needed the time alone to think and get past the sudden emptiness they were experiencing.

Taylor had never really felt loneliness, at least not as a burden, but now that Estelle was gone, he couldn't stop thinking of her. Was she alright, was she home safe, and lastly, was she alone? That last thought drove him mad. He did not like this Dan guy and he blamed him for taking her away so quickly, without proper time to say goodbye and to prepare.

"I don't even have her number, what an idiot," he muttered to himself as he stuck the pitchfork in the pile of hay of Shakespeare's shed.

His hands were full of blisters now as he had been relentlessly working and not having felt the exhaustion and physical pains he was enduring. His mind being entirely preoccupied. It all went so fast.

"Come on Taylor, wake up," said Samuel as he found him asleep in the shed, pitchfork still fast in his hand.

Taylor could hardly pull himself out of his sleep, part of him was conscious that Samuel was trying to get him up to take him home but he could not respond. No limbs in his body would obey him. He could not pull himself out of the tight grip of exhaustion. After a few maneuvers, Samuel managed to get him onto his shoulder and carried him to his room with some difficulty. Taylor could hear Samuel's every word and move. He felt Samuel undress him and clean his hands and face and tuck him into his bed. He also felt his worry. Worry that he had not fallen ill. Samuel stayed by his side all night. Checking up on him every now and then until he too gave in to Morpheus.

The house stood strong amidst the frozen winds that circled and embraced its sides. The night crawled by unnaturally as if it too were feeling the same emptiness its two inhabitants were. All three slept of not a true sleep and not a true wake, somewhere in between both worlds. They were in "slake", A place where dreams could not come distinctly, just a hazy and vague impression of a dream yet nothing. A mirage of a dream. The bodies were asleep but the minds would not give in.

Taylor was pulled out of his semi-sleep startled by a sound he could not recognize. He got up and passed Samuel, who was asleep in the armchair next to the bed. The sound came from Estelle's room. The thought of her being back did cross his mind and intensified as he approached the door. He stood in front of it, his hand reaching out to the knob but unable to touch it. The closer his hand approached to grab it the further the door seemed to be. This puzzled him and he tried over and over again. He could hear footsteps and moving around on the other side. He finally called out, "Estelle? Is that you? Are you back?" But there was no answer, he called her name out, again and again, each time a little louder and filled with frustration.

All of a sudden, the door slid away from him and opened up to a room he had never seen. He saw Estelle sitting next to a fireplace, staring into it, her cheeks shining from the tears she had not wiped off. He had never seen her so sad and ab-sorbed. He tried to go near her but the same distance sep-arated him from her the more he walked towards her. The room was dim and she turned to him and looked into his eyes begging for him to come closer. He couldn't, no matter how hard he tried. He felt a force pushing him back against his chest, he tried to resist it.

"Taylor," a familiar voice murmured as hands gently shook his chest to awaken him.

As Taylor opened his eyes and no longer saw the dim room with Estelle in it but Sheriff Allister's worried face right in front of him he realized he had been dreaming.

"You alright son?" Allister asked in a fatherly tone.

Taylor nodded as he scratched his head and turned to look at the time. It was 12:10 pm. He never overslept.

"I'm okay, I think I crashed out of exhaustion last night."

"I bet you did, it's been quite the week," Allister answered as he took his hat off and sat back into the armchair Samuel had been sleeping in during the night.

"You know you can take more days off since it's been so hectic for you, with the accident and the girl. You should have some time for yourself before you come back."

Taylor looked at him blankly and couldn't make up his mind, whether he'd be better off working to forget about everything or take more time off to sort things out.

"Well, you don't have to make up your mind straight away, don't worry. Just come back whenever you feel like it. It's pretty calm so no rush," Allister added calmly scrutinizing Taylor's every expression.

Taylor nodded and thanked Allister for his patience and kindness.

"Well, have some rest and give me some news, I have to run," Allister said as he got up and adjusted his hat and jacket.

Taylor lay in bed for a while, not knowing what to get up for. Nothing motivated him. He wasn't tired nor hungry. Even the usual craving for coffee couldn't shake him out of bed. His eyes wandered around the room with distant memories here and there of various things just flashing through his head. There was no noise in the house, no smell either. The emptiness gained him again. He did not want to let it get to him again. He had to find something to do. Maybe he should go back to work after all. Maybe it was the remedy to all this.

He finally got up and put some pants on. He lazily walked through the living room and into the kitchen. Nothing had been touched. The dirty dishes from yesterday's last breakfast with Estelle were still in the kitchen sink. There was some leftover coffee that he poured into a mug and placed into the microwave. He was surprised how there was no tangible trace of her anywhere. How someone who filled up the house as much as she had could just vanish without a trace. He might even have dreamt all of it.

After having coffee and a dried-up piece of toast, he cleaned up the whole kitchen until it was immaculate. He showered and changed into his riding clothes and took Shakespeare out. Fresh air and scenery could only do him good.

The frozen air struck him but he embraced it. He loved the cold, the icy cold particles on his cheeks and nose. His eyes watered from it. He saddled Shakespeare and got up on him swiftly. The snow was still several inches deep. Each hoof drew a hole in the trail as a cracking sound preceded each step. Shakespeare was frisky from the cold and lack of exercise. He longed to gallop into the backcountry but Taylor restrained him until they got to the prairie to avoid any sprains and falls.

The prairie was shining with the sun's reflection in the virgin white plains. Taylor finally let Shakespeare gallop through the prairie for as much as he wanted, he let him guide and pace the rhythm. Taylor let him lead from there on and let nature and surroundings penetrate him, refuel him. When they both started to get tired they set back towards the house at a slow but steady pace. The night was starting to fall, the sky was orangish pink as they approached the shed.

There were no new footsteps in the path and no new car in the driveway. As Taylor entered the house he thought he'd see Samuel on the couch waiting for him but the house was empty. There was no sign of Samuel. Taylor did not think about it and went to take a bath to warm up before he would make dinner and prepare to watch a movie, no matter what. He set his program and followed every step of it. He had dinner in front of his TV and fireplace. Nothing crossed his mind, the fresh air had emptied his thoughts and he had returned to his normal self before all that had happened.

He felt reassured and confident he had managed to outplay the recent changes in his habits. The day and night passed on a positively satisfactory note.

No dreams or noises had visited him that night.

| 24 |

"I'm fine mom. I was just away in the countryside. I had no reception and no phone intentionally to be able to work on new material. You know how it is. I just don't know why you worry like you do all of a sudden," Estelle dryly said to her mother who had woken her up at 4 am.

"You can't leave me without news for so long, I get worried. Why didn't you tell me you were going out of town? It's the least you could do. You know you are so far away, it's not that easy for me," her mother argued.

"I know Mom, I'm sorry. It was not planned, it was the spur-of-the-moment thing and then it was too late. But you have to realize that I am a big girl now, I can take care of myself. You do not have to be checking up on me like this and get insanely worried just because I'm not answering your calls. Seriously."

"We'll talk about it again the day you have children," her mother interrupted.

Estelle did not answer that.

"Ok, Mom, it's 4 am, now that you know I'm alive, can I go back to sleep the few hours I have left before I have to get up and go to work."

"Good night, honey, I love you."

"Love you too," Estelle replied coldly and hung up.

She let her head crash hard onto her pillow releasing a heavy sigh. She looked at the time and despised her mother for having called her that early. She tossed and turned and fell back asleep quicker than she'd imagined. Before she could finish her dream the ringing of the alarm pulled her out of it without her being able to reach Taylor. She had seen him come into the room and she wanted him to come closer but she could not move and he would not approach. This made her feel like calling sick for the day and going back to sleep, back to that same moment in her dream but she knew Dan would get angry.

With all that had just happened, she was in no position to play around anymore. The time she had been able to be away felt so unbelievable as if she had dreamt it all. As if she were now waking from that dream, back into reality. She reasoned herself as she got up and went down to the kitchen and made coffee. She sat in front of the news as she lit a cigarette and drank her coffee black. She stared into the screen but the images and words did not pass into her conscience. She just needed the company. She wasn't listening and did not want to hear what horrible things were happening to others. She was not at a place in her life where she wanted to relate. She was self-absorbed and completely aware of it.

The doorbell made her jump and lose her half-smoked cigarette.

"Shit," she cursed in a low voice as she picked it back up as quick as she could from the cream-colored carpet.

"Just a minute," she yelled out to the door.

She ran to the door and looked through the window. It was Dan. She opened the door and let him in.

"Hey," he said as he came inside.

"Hi, sorry I'm a little slow this morning," she answered.

"There's no rush," he said as he followed her into the kitchen and watched her pour him a cup of coffee.

"So, what's the program," she asked and lit the rest of her cigarette.

"Well, we have to prepare that interview for the radio, for one and then Spencer wants us to all have a little meeting to discuss things."

Estelle nodded and continued sipping her coffee and staring at the screen.

"Are you feeling better, did you have a good sleep?" he asked.

"Not too bad," she said her eyes still glued to the news report.

"I'm going to go get ready. I'll be quick, she said as she popped back into the conversation and jumped to her feet with motivation.

She ran up the stairs and undressed on the way. She stepped into the shower and the cold water ran down her face and body, the goosebumps covered every inch of her and her breath would stop every time the cold hit her chest. She loved cold showers in the morning and was quite used to them now. She got ready faster than Dan had expected and before he finished preparing some notes to go through she was there before him, as fresh and beautiful as ever.

"Let's go out for breakfast and go through the notes there," she suggested as she was now starving and had nothing in her fridge.

Estelle had so dreaded and feared this re-adjustment to her life but everything was going smoothly and she didn't even feel pain or regret. She thought she would be incapable of leaving Blackmont. She had persuaded herself that her life was meaningless and empty but none of this now appeared to her. She had popped back into herself. As if that other Estelle, the one in Blackmont were a different version of her. She saw all her memories of her thoughts and feelings as if they were strangers now. She did not recognize herself. It was only yesterday that she left but it already all seemed like a distant memory.

The city had adopted her back into its womb. She had countless emails she had to answer now that she was back. Dan had already prioritized some of them. They calmly and vividly went through the different questions and Estelle was back to her professional self, involved and passionate again. She had put aside Dan's advances before the entire incident and was dealing with it well in her opinion. Dan too was reassured that the collaboration they had built all these months had not been shot to pieces on such an account.

Dan drove Estelle to the rental company so she could pick

up a new rental he then followed her back to her apartment and they scheduled the next day.

"You should still take it easy for the next few days. We'll catch up all the work little by little, no need to rush things," he told her as she opened the passenger door.

"I'm fine, Dan, really. Don't worry," she answered smiling as she bent over his car window. She waved him goodbye as he backed out and drove off.

She came inside and locked the door, kicked off her boots, and undressed. Turned the news on again and lit a cigarette. She lay on the couch and stared at the ceiling as the news floated through the room and entwined with the smoke she exhaled.

She relaxed on the couch, lulled by the reporter's monotonous voice, she began feeling lighter and felt herself consciously sinking into slumber. She found herself in the woods. At that same place, she had seen Koko. The place was empty and dark. She walked around to search for Koko and listened closely to hear any sound that could be hers. But there was nothing but silence. She was walking in circles always back to where she had stood at the beginning. There were trails but she could not take them. She was now tired of the dream but it would not disappear until she was woken by the sound of her doorbell. It took her a few seconds to realize someone had really rung her doorbell. She painfully got up and walked to the door and looked through the peephole. She couldn't believe her eyes.

| 25 |

Dan was relieved of the turn of events. He had feared losing Estelle. Those past few days had been pure torture for him. He could finally sit back and relax and that was exactly what he had in mind. He parked his car and got home to a freshly cleaned house, his maid had just left. She had put the pile of mail he had not yet opened on the dining-room table. He ignored it and went to the kitchen and grabbed a beer from the fridge and comfortably sat in front of the baseball game. He wasn't even really watching it but his mind was not thinking of anything else, he was exhausted. Exhausted from the worry, the drive, and his emotions.

His phone rang, it was his ex-wife's number. She had already tried calling three times but the last thing he had the strength for was a conversation with her. He let it ring until it went to voicemail and then he put his phone on silent mode. He thought of Estelle and how she had surprised him jumping back into the game as if nothing had ever happened. From their argument to the accident. Not one word about any of it. It was the best way to get past it and he felt satisfied and ready to move on. He remembered her reaction when he entered the house the day before. The anger and disappointment. He thought she would never leave and go back with him. It was a risky thing to do but he was glad it worked out in his favor.

He couldn't stop thinking of what had happened to her during those days staying in that house with two strangers. He couldn't help but notice how close they all seemed. What could have brought them that close together in such little time? They both seemed very disappointed to see her go. Especially the Indian type man. He was austere and cold. Dan spent his evening imagining possible scenarios and surprised himself feeling a hint of jealousy. He was dying to know but it was the last thing he could talk to Estelle about. He knew the grounds for their pursued collaboration were not solid. Time had to pass before he could even mention anything about the whole episode. He knew that and it obsessed him.

Estelle, whether he wanted it or not had become the center of his life. Every morning up until the evening she was in his mind. How could one not become close and lose ground, no matter how professional one can be it is human nature to get attached. No matter how much he tried to persuade himself he couldn't be detached, he couldn't. There he was, alone at home relaxing, and still, all he could think about was her. Maybe it was time for him to start seeing someone, maybe he was obsessing over Estelle just because he had no other woman around to think about, to care about.

He had drunk three beers and had fallen asleep on the couch once more. He hardly ever slept in his bed, he hated sleeping in an empty bedroom. The television kept him company through his lonely nights. The alcohol helped him as well. He would not drink much in public. He was serious when it came to business. But when he got home, it was always the same thing. He had to have a drink. And with the drink came the thoughts, and with the thoughts came the regrets and remorse until he gave into slumber and forgot everything about it in the morning.

| **26** |

The sun burned his cheek as he woke up that morning. He had slept a heavy sleep and felt fresh and eager to make the most of his day. It was 9:00 am. He jumped out of bed and fixed himself a quick breakfast. He started to wonder how Samuel was, he realized he hadn't seen him since the day Estelle left and that hazy night when he had disappeared. He decided to check Estelle's room to see if he had slept there. The room was empty and the bed as it had been left the morning she had left.

Taylor wasn't really worried; he was used to Samuel's volatile ways. He was just surprised he'd left him alone just as he had after Koko's death. Taylor could not stay indoors another whole day. He felt eager to be doing something as if he wanted to escape something. He thought he should probably go back to work, there was no point in staying home if it were to lay around the house with nothing specific to do. He had had enough of it and decided to get a move on.

He took a quick warm shower, grabbed his uniform, and ironed it as fast as he could trying to focus on work. As he left and shut the front door behind him, without locking up he looked around the path to see if there were any footsteps but there weren't. He earnestly jumped into his car and blasted the stereo, pulled out of the driveway, and drove to town. He was feeling relaxed and happy to be back on the road. He drove past the spot the accident had taken place and it had been covered up by fresh snow, he could not even notice anything had ever happened. He thought how strange it was that things could change so quickly without a trace. How the emptiness felt so familiar to him, but he did have a strange feeling creeping upon him. Flowing through his veins and silently taking possession of him.

He did his best to ignore it but he knew that in time that feeling was going to explode him right in the face when he would least be expecting and prepared for it. His eyes focused on the snowy road and the song playing on the radio. He felt a twitch in his upper lip, the more he approached the town the stiffer he was feeling. His hands clutched the wheel as if he needed to control the vehicle. A roaring deafening sound came from the car. He did not know where it came from nor what he had to do so he continued to town and stopped at the garage to have it checked.

As he drove into the garage his friend smiled and walked right up to him.

"Taylor, man, what does me the honor?" he said laughing and giving Taylor a big friendly hug.

"Hey, glad to see you, pal. I don't know I was driving down and all of a sudden she made a roaring sound, nothing I've ever heard before. Thought it was best you took a look."

"Ok, let's see," he answered as he looked under the hood.

As he inspected the truck through and through, both men talked over all the things they hadn't had a chance to tell each other, and after a good two hours checking Sean said:

"Can't find anything wrong with her, she's like new. Maybe it was from outside."

Taylor looked skeptical but completely trusted his friend's diagnosis. Taylor thanked him and said they should not wait as long before they catch up again.

As he got back into his truck and turned the key, the engine started and the radio was playing a voice that caught Taylor's ear. He couldn't quite make out who was singing, he didn't know the song but the voice felt so very familiar. He listened to the entire song and was anxiously waiting for the singer's name.

"You are on KCWT and that was Estelle Blanc's single "Diamond Eyes". Coming up next on …".

Taylor's ears stopped listening, it couldn't be. The emptiness he was feeling just grew deeper. He couldn't ignore this feeling, he hoped to bury it deep like he had done when Koko passed away but Estelle was alive. Just miles away. It wasn't the same. As he arrived and parked at work he sat behind the wheel and stared out to the sheriff's sign over the door. His hands were still firmly gripping the stirring-wheel, his lips were pinched and his wide eyes hadn't blinked for so long that they were watering down on his cheekbones. He held tight as his grief tried to pour out and escape. He had never shown his feelings to anyone, he didn't want to start to now. He waited in the truck for it to pass before he walked through the office door.

As he walked in Gayle, the secretary, greeted him with a warm smile.

"Taylor! Glad to see you! Sheriff Allister is in his office. Do you want some coffee?" she asked as she stood up and walked to the coffee machine.

"Hi, I would love that, thank you, Gayle," he kindly answered as he walked towards Allister's office and knocked lightly at the door."

"Come in," said the voice inside the office.

"Taylor, son," Allister stood and held his arms up to embrace him.

"Welcome back."

The familiar old and brownish decoration he had known for years, every inch of every file and frame hanging on the walls made him feel in a safe and secure space as if he were home. He walked into his office, as tidy as he had left it. Sat at his desk and reached out to the cup of coffee Gayle had brought him. He inspected every corner of his office as he sipped his coffee slowly, getting the feel of the place back. Wondering where he had left off, everything felt so blurry, as if it were another lifetime. He watched the clock arrow go round and round. He got nothing done, he didn't even open the file that was on his desk. He just sat there for hours. The phone never rang and no one came in until Gayle appeared at the door.

"If you don't need anything, I'm done for the day," she said half-questioningly, half hoping he wouldn't ask for something so she could head home.

"No, I'm fine Gayle, thank you. Have a good evening."

"Thank you, glad you're back Taylor." She said as she walked away and the front door opened and closed behind her.

Taylor had been sitting in his office for five straight hours staring at the walls. He couldn't make himself decide to go home. He was somehow waiting for something to turn up but nothing did. The calmness hadn't weighed on him before. He started feeling restless but still wouldn't budge when an idea popped up in his mind. He turned his computer on and opened Google. He typed in the name Estelle Blanc and paused before clicking search. Her ID said Estelle Lenoir but maybe it was her stage name or something. He finally hit search and saw Estelle's face pop up in front of him. It startled him at first as he enlarged the photo. He recognized her but she seemed. different, the make-up and photo reflected too much sophistication and glamour but not the girl he had fallen in love with. His fingers touched the screen and he ran them down her cheek.

She didn't look comfortable with herself in the photo, the assurance she was told to incarnate on contrary rendered the opposite. He felt her fragility more than he had ever when she was flesh and bone by his side. But still, she was beautiful. He spent hours going through various photos, articles, reviews, clicking away to gather every possible detail he could about her. He learned she was French which explained the VISA but that her mother was an English teacher who had always spoken to her in English. The more he read the more he wanted to read but everything was so professional, he needed something more intimate. Her twitter hadn't been updated in a while and the only tweets there was news about her music. He couldn't access her Facebook as he didn't have an account. He had never needed one. Every person he knew, he saw at work every day so no need for virtual communication. He had, of course, heard of it but had no clue how to go about with it. Just when he was about to click "create an account" a voice startled him.

"You planning on staying here all night or coming to dinner at ours?" Allister's kind voice broke the eight-hour-long silence he had been tucked in.

"Sure, that's a wonderful idea," Taylor answered turning his screen off and walking up to the door behind Allister before Allister had time to approach his desk. He didn't want him to know he had been spending his entire day on the internet looking for information about Estelle. How would it look? Work was work, even if Allister and he were close, there were boundaries he would not cross.

| **27** |

She unlocked the door.

"Samuel? What are you doing here? How did you find me?" she said surprised and confused.

"Can I come in?" he answered.

"Of course," she answered showing him in and looking outside to see if there was anyone else before closing the door behind her.

"Taylor's not with me," Samuel said noticing her quick search.

"Sorry I didn't expect to see you. What brings you here?" she asked again a little worried. "Is everything alright?"

Samuel quietly sat down on her sofa. He lay back and looked around the room. She knew her place seemed more like a hotel room than a proper home. There was no decoration, no personal touch and it wasn't cozy nor welcoming. The place was empty and cold and the furniture was contemporary and scarce. He could tell she didn't spend much time there. Nothing there reminded him of her.

Estelle was starting to get tired of waiting for Samuel to finally start talking so she went over to the kitchen making some noise and came back with two cups of coffee. She put one of them in front of Samuel and keeping hers in her hand she sat down in front of him.

"So, are you going to tell me what this is all about?" she asked staring him in the eyes.

He leaned over and pushed the coffee away. He took hers away from her to be able to hold her hands in his. This closeness startled Estelle. She was wondering what had taken over him.

His eyes were so piercing and hypnotizing that she could not turn away nor even blink. Her heart started pounding as if his pulse was beating into her body.

"You've got to come back," were his words.

Estelle felt a heavy weight push down on her shoulders. His low steady voice still echoing in her ears and his pulse beating through her body like drums.

"Sam, I can't, I have a life here and a lot of work to get done. I've already missed out on many things and I have to make up for it," she insisted.

Samuel let go of her hands coldly and lay back on the sofa. The release was harsh and she could still feel the warmth of his touch slowly evaporating. The fire in his eyes was contained but the static energy he released filled up the entire room and Estelle didn't know what to say nor do. She grabbed his hands and sat on her knees right in front of him. He made no effort.

"Sam, I know it's hard for you, I know how you feel, but I just don't think there is a solution to all this. The things that happened were so unreal, so unexplainable, that I can't just leave my life behind in the pursuit of a ghost. I know it's your sister and that you wish she had come to you instead of me. I'm sorry." She went on trying to make eye contact.

Samuel did not speak nor look at her. His hands tightened together in a clutch. She squeezed his hands in hers. They were twice the size of hers.

"You will come back, when, I don't know but you will. You have to, you are linked to her now, as long as she needs you. I just want to be here by your side through the whole process. I want to help you through this because it's not all that simple to deal with. It's not because you left Blackmont that Blackmont has let you go."

His words rang in her head, bouncing endlessly from one side to the other. If what he was saying was true, she was trapped, wherever she went, no matter what she did. The thought of it made her suffocate. Samuel picked her up and held her in his arms to calm her down. She had forgotten how warm he was. She let his warmth invade her. He was her shelter through the storm. A solid rock she could lean on. In a way, she was glad he had come to her. She liked to feel protected, from what she didn't know. She wanted to ask about Taylor but she didn't want to break the feel of the moment. She wondered how true what Samuel had said was. Would she still be under Koko's power even miles away? She had the impression Koko let her go. She hadn't felt anything strange since she returned to Seattle. Did Samuel just say that so she would be afraid? So that she would go back to Blackmont. The questions danced around as she was half asleep in Samuel's arms.

"It's so good to see you again. My, how you look exhausted!" Mrs. Allister said as she opened the door to greet them and helped Taylor take his coat off.

The warm heat of the fireplace embraced Taylor in a second and his mind was finally starting to switch off from his afternoon obsessions. Being in the Allister house again made him feel like a child going to his grandparents'. The table was set for the three of them near the fireplace.

"Well, the boy's had quite the week," Tim said in response to his wife, Alice.

"So I heard. Poor boy, those weren't really holidays but more of a nightmare I must say. Craziest story I've heard in years. And I've seen a few years pass by," Alice said her hand on her chest still smiling gently.

"Well, never mind that now, it's all over. I'm sure Tim will let you take a proper vacation when you decide to," she continued looking at Tim as she went to the kitchen to bring a bottle of wine and handed it over to Tim to open.

"I already told the boy he didn't have to come back until he felt like it. But he turned up this morning regardless," Tim said as the cork popped out.

No one talked as the wine was being poured into all three glasses. Tim handed the glasses out and Alice raised her glass and looked at Taylor.

"To a well-deserved break," she said smiling and winked at Taylor.

The wine felt nice and warm going down his throat and at the third sip he started feeling the warmness run through his entire body. He was feeling relaxed sitting there next to the fire. The dinner was nice and refreshing compared to all the things he had been through the past few days. The change of scenery and company eased him. It kept his mind off things.

"Well, I think I should be getting myself back home now before I fall asleep," Taylor said smiling and folding his napkin and placing it under his cup of coffee.

"Oh, well, you can stay here for the night if you feel too tired to drive back. You know it's not a problem," Tim said.

"Thanks, that's nice of you but I'm fine. The drive will do me some good."

"As you wish but you drive carefully now," said Alice in a worried voice.

"Don't you start worrying, I've done this a million times," Taylor answered as he gave her a thankful hug.

He hugged Tim as well, then put his coat on and opened the door.

The cold hit him like a whip. He ran to his truck and closed the door as fast as he could as if it would help. The truck was freezing cold inside as well. He turned the heater up and waited a minute before pulling back from the driveway. The air was freezing but there was no wind. The street was deserted and dark. The truck broke the peaceful serenity as if roared past the crossroads and sleeping homes. His heart always paced a little each time he approached the scene of the accident. Secretly hoping, wishing he could live that moment over and over again. But there was nothing there, no sign of her. He drove away slowly.

| 29 |

"Samuel has disappeared."

"Good let's hope it stays that way, it's better he stays far from Taylor," replied the other voice over the receiver.

"Looks like he's been gone since the girl has left. Maybe he's after her after all."

"Maybe, but let's not push aside the other possibility."

"I'll keep my eyes and ears open."

"Same here."

| 30 |

Estelle's palms were sweaty and her throat was dry. Dan's hands started massaging her. Her neck was stiff. They were standing outside of Spencer's office. Dan had the masters of the studio sessions ready.

"Relax, it's going to be fine, Estelle. Trust me," he whispered in her ear.

The door opened and a tall skinny lady in her early forties said: "Spencer is ready for you." And she let them in.

Dan made a sign for Estelle to go in as he followed close behind.

"Estelle, good to see you again," Spencer said smiling as he stood to greet her.

"Dan, good to see you too. Have a seat. So I heard about your accident," Spencer continued looking at Estelle.

"I hope you're feeling better, we were all very worried about you here."

"Thank you, Spencer, I imagine how worried you all must've been but I'm fine now," she replied shyly.

"Well, that's the past now. Dan let's get down to it. Shall we. I can't wait to hear the new material, the single was excellent and it's doing extremely well as you might already know."

Dan stood and handed Spencer the CD. Spencer walked up to the listening parlor and asked both of them to come sit next to him in front of the speakers. Once all three were comfortably seated Spencer pressed play.

Estelle couldn't stand it, the pressure was at its highest. She tried to take a peek at Spencer's face without it being obvious just so she could see his reaction. She hesitated but finally, her eyes met his. She noticed a smile stretching over the sides of his lips and his eyes were sparkling. All the weight she had felt just before lifted off at that sight. She breathed in deeply and smiled back bashfully.

Spencer listened through the entire five tracks and at the end of the last one he clapped his hands heavily. He was very enthusiastic, she had not expected that from him. He had always seemed so distant and serious.

Estelle could read the confidence freshly arisen in Dan's posture. Dan pointed at Estelle and said: "It's all her doing."

"I must say, this is great work. Dan I don't regret giving you the go on this one, I have to admit, you've always had the nose for these things. I don't know how you do it, but you do it."

"So, is that a "yes" to continue the record or what?" Dan asked sharply.

Estelle was put back on such a familiar attack on Dan's part. He sure knew what he was doing.

"It's more than a go, take everything you need, time and budget-wise," Spencer replied.

Dan thanked Spencer with a friendly handshake and a hug and turned to hug Estelle grabbing her by the shoulders and turning her around so that she was facing Spencer. Spencer took her hands and kissed them and said: "good job, keep it up, I'm impatient to hear more." Estelle blushed and thanked him.

"Let's go for lunch, it's on me," Spencer suggested as he called his secretary and asked her to book a table for them right away.

All three had lunch in a hype restaurant downtown. Spencer was the happiest man she'd seen in ages. His energy and wholehearted laughs seemed alien to her. Dan managed well to keep him entertained during the entire meal. All in all, it was a pleasant moment; no matter how unexpected it had been for Estelle. She was glad he had not asked details about the accident. She was happy the day was on a bright note. When they finished lunch Spencer took them back to Dan's car. He congratulated Estelle again for the great work. She liked him, he wasn't the pushy type nor the condescending type, and it suited her well since she had trouble pretending.

"Well, that went more than well, didn't it?" Dan said to Estelle as he was driving her back to her place.

"Yeah, I still can't believe it," she replied, her eyes staring out on the road.

"I told you there was nothing to be worried about. I know the guy so well; it's like reading a book for the twentieth time," he said and chuckled.

"Anyway, you know what this means, right? It's all up to you now, you need to be writing new material and fast."

"Yup, it's all up to me," she answered hoping deep down inside that she was capable of it.

"So, I need you to be sending me at least one new song a day. Ok? And then we'll go from there, once I think we've got what it takes I'll book the producer and studio." Dan had his business talk voice on. She had heard more of that at the beginning of their relationship but was a bit surprised to hear it again after such a long time. He knew she needed some sort of pressure to be productive.

Dan forced himself to talk to her like that, he knew it would get her going, pinching her soft spot. He had finally found the right tone, not too pushy so she wouldn't completely shut her out and make her run away again and not too smooth so that she wouldn't care and procrastinate.

"There you are princess," he said as he parked in front of her place.

"Thank you, Dan. Thank you for everything, I know this is all thanks to you." She hugged him briefly and got out of the car. She waved him goodbye as she watched him drive away.

Dan was still surprised, Estelle had never thanked him, not like that. It touched him and he felt satisfied with the way things had actually worked out. A week ago everything was on the verge of crumbling, all downhill and now everything was looking up. He couldn't have asked for more. Well, maybe, but that was ruled out for the moment. At the red light, he checked his phone and saw his ex-wife had tried to call five times.

"Linda, seriously, give me a break," he mumbled out to himself as he was driving back home.

His phone rang again and he decided to answer.

"Linda," he said.

"It's about time, I've been trying to get a hold of you for days. Not easy," she said slightly angry and annoyed.

"I've got a lot on my shoulders, what's so important?" he answered.

"You know that exposition I talked to you about, I want you to be there, it's tonight."

"Oh, right, already. Ok just text me the address and time and I'll come by."

"See you tonight," she said and hung up.

Not the type of evening Dan had in mind but he couldn't say no to Linda, he never could. He was not at all into painting and he hated her friends but there would be plenty of alcohol so he decided he would take a taxi to get there and back home. Why she wanted him to be there, he still couldn't understand. Every time they talked or saw each other she was cold and distant. He had no pleasure in her company and even wondered how he had ever been able to have any. Of course, she was beautiful but so self-centered. Her inner ugliness had forever stained her outer beauty in his eyes but still when she asked, she got.

When Estelle got home she wondered if Samuel would still be there but the minute she stepped in she saw him sitting at her kitchen table, it seemed like he was studying. He had half a dozen books opened in front of him and he was taking notes. He knew she was home but he pretended to be surprised when he lifted his head and met her questioning eyes. She couldn't help but notice how bad an actor he was. It was almost comic. Estelle ignored it and held back her teasing grin.

"Hey." He finally lifted his nose out of his book to look at her swiftly then put it straight back in, absorbed by what he was doing.

"Hey. I see you've been to the library. What are you up to?" she questioned curiously.

"Oh, just doing some research."

"Hey, that part I can see, it's pretty obvious, but what kind of research may I ask?"

"Just stuff."

"Alright, it seems like pretty intense stuff but I trust you will tell me when you want to so I'll just go on upstairs and work. If you need anything let me know," she answered half annoyed half nonchalant.

"Sure," was his long and developed response that spiked the hair on Estelle's body.

As she went up the stairs to her studio, well not exactly a proper studio, just a room she dedicated to music, she remembered how long it had been since she'd been in there. The dust on her keyboard and guitars confirmed her long absence from them. She felt embarrassed, remembering how much she had longed for all this, and then now that she had it in close range she was trying to escape from it. She didn't understand, why she was reacting like that.

She pulled herself together and decided to give herself a

big hard kick and get herself back in the game. She'd had more than enough time to process, now she had to spit it all out. At least one song a day. It seemed impossible. She felt she hadn't been able to write a new song in months. So how was she supposed to get one song out a day? She desperately ravaged her notebooks to see if she had anything to start on. She went through notebook after notebook, page after page. None of the words she had written seemed to be her.

"Crap, there's nothing good," she said in despair throwing the last notebook back into its box.

She lay down on the floor and stared at the ceiling. She got drowsy, closed her eyes, and let her body sink into the carpet.

Taylor's alarm rang out for the third time but he still couldn't make it out of his sleep. He had had trouble finding sleep all night and now he was struggling to get out of it. He hated the feeling of not being in control. He was the type to be up at the break of dawn waiting for it to be time to leave the house. He had never had trouble sleeping before but these past few nights had been horrible. The silence he was so accustomed to was now unbearable. Every crack in the house, every squeak of the floors, every gust of wind made him wait expecting something more but there was nothing more. He would lay in his bed for hours just waiting for something to happen but nothing did. His eyes were bloated and red from the lack of sleep, he had to have some sleep. He couldn't go back to the office looking like that, Allister would worry and the last thing he wanted was to have Allister on his back.

He finally found the strength to get out of bed, grabbed his robe, and walked to the kitchen. As he passed the empty living room and looked at the cold fireplace he felt depressed nothing had moved, nothing had changed, everything was right where it had been since Estelle had left. He hated feeling that way, out of control and full of emotion, this state he had always fought against, reminiscent of his old wounds and the scars they had left. And Samuel again was nowhere near him, he had no one to talk to or share his solitude with, just like the last time.

He rummaged through his kitchen cupboards but didn't find enough coffee for breakfast. As if things weren't bad enough. He had been so absorbed by everything that had been going on that he had lost track of the other things. He hadn't cleaned the place either. It just didn't feel like home anymore. He couldn't explain why.

He showered and got ready to leave the house. He needed to run some errands and get things back a flow. Before taking off he fed Shakespeare and cleaned his stall. He decided he'd be driving to Missoula to get a change of scenery. He had given Gayle a call to tell her he wouldn't be coming in after all. Once he got a list of everything he needed for the house he set out. The truck was cold but warmed up by the morning sun. He turned the engine on and the radio set to the same channel he had heard Estelle on hoping he would hear her again. The snow had thawed and the roads were a lot better.

He hadn't driven out of Blackmont in months. The last time was to get a new water heater for the house, not the most exciting errand. It was a two-and-a-half-hour drive but he didn't mind. He knew Estelle had been driving this road a few days ago to go back to Seattle. It even passed his mind to keep driving until he reached her but he didn't even know where she lived. He didn't even have her number... He stopped at the next gas station to fill up the tank and grab some coffee for the remainder of the drive. He was now about half-way. He also asked the worker to clean the truck. The rest of the drive was pleasant and smooth. It was strange for him to see so many cars and people all of a sudden.

He stopped for a quick lunch and then started shopping. He bought new clothes, books, music, and DVDs. He got some things for Shakespeare and the house. He also bought a new laptop. He hesitated to get a new mobile phone but it was useless as there was almost no use for it. He passed by a music store and decided to have a look. After an hour in the acoustic guitar aisle, he decided to ask the salesman for some help. He ended up getting a baby Taylor just because he liked the idea.

All that done he went to the supermarket and got all the groceries he needed and even more. He was back home after sunset and felt satisfied with his day. He got everything out of the truck. The new clothes that he momentarily put on his bed and the guitar beside them. He fixed himself a sandwich and popcorn. He sat on the couch in front of the fire and took the laptop out of its box and started installing everything. He was not good at these things so it did take him quite some time but he got an Apple computer, as advised by the seller. And he was surprised how simple and fast everything was compared to his old PC.

When he finished all he could do on the laptop he turned

it off and grabbed one of the books he had just bought and started reading away. Hours passed by and sleep still didn't call for him. Halfway through the book, he was interrupted by a sudden feeling of intense cold. The fire was still well off and blazing but he felt a gush of freezing air surrounding him. He looked towards the windows and door to see if anything was open but nothing was. He sat there wondering what it could be expecting to hear something.

After a few minutes, he pulled over the plaid that was on the couch and started reading again. A few pages further the lights started dimming and the cold intensified. He was now seeing steam coming out of his mouth as he exhaled. He was starting to feel very uncomfortable. He frantically looked around the room reluctant to move a limb just in case it triggered something more. He then heard a door squeak, it came from Estelle's room.

He finally decided to get up and check. As he turned into the hallway the door was wide open. He peeked inside and saw nothing. As he walked in to make sure he hadn't missed something he heard something fall to the floor. He looked around and there was a notebook. He bent over to pick it up. It was one of Estelle's notebooks. It must have fallen out of her purse when she was packing. He was glad to have found it. He took another glance at the room and walked out, he closed the door behind him. He held the notebook preciously and put it on the living room coffee table. He sat back on the couch and grabbed his book. He opened it to where he had left off to find the page covered with charcoal writing. It read:
"SAVE ME"
He dropped the book instantly and looked around the

room in a panic, his heart stopped. He looked around to see what he could grab to strike someone. He grabbed the silver candle holder. He moved slowly to make the least noise possible as he inspected the house. After tiptoeing through the entire house he yelled:

"Who's there? Stop hiding, come out and show yourself!"

No reply except heavy silence and the crackling wood burning in the fireplace.

Taylor felt ridiculous and shaky. After long minutes just standing there waiting for another strange event, he noticed the night had slipped by, the sun was rising and the first orange-colored glow was filling the room. He went to the kitchen like a robot and made coffee, he would need a lot. He made scrambled eggs, bacon, and toast. He was starving from exhaustion or rattled emotions. His mind was blank, he mechanically ate his breakfast and drank his coffee.

The sun warmed the house in no time. It was 7 am and he had had no sleep. He couldn't decide if he should try to go to bed or just move on with his day until he collapsed. He tried to lay in bed but tossed and turned. He called Gayle again to tell, her he still wouldn't be coming in. She was sweet. He liked her but she was married and had three children already. He stared out the window from his bed not able to sleep but not wanting to get up either when he remembered about the notebook. He got up to get it, it was still on the coffee table. He grabbed it and went back to his bed. He smelled it to see if it smelled like her, and it did a little. He inspected it closely before he let into opening it.

The cover was damaged and washed out. The pages were

wrinkled and the ink was faded in certain areas. The writing was messy and not always decipherable. He read through random words, sometimes with interest and others just flying over the sentences without much attention. One particular draft caught his attention:

On a lonely road in the middle of nowhere
I found myself when I got lost
I found you, you, my mysterious host
Stranded in this icy air

Discovering the warmth under the frost
Where does it end
And where does it begin?
I can no longer pretend
So I stand here begging you to

Let me in
Let me into you
Let me in
Let me inside you

You let me in and gave meaning to my life
I let you in the cracks of my heart
Fearing the day we would be torn apart
Like the strike of a knife

I felt there was something right from the start

Why did it end
And why did it begin?
I could no longer pretend
And I should've stood there begging you to

Keep me in
Keep me into you
Keep me in
Keep me inside you

Taylor couldn't believe his eyes. Every word connected back to what happened. Had she seen this in a dream or was it pure coincidence? The thought meandered in his mind. What if everything happened for a reason? What if everything were written and we only choose to follow or not to follow the signs?

| 32 |

Estelle felt her body sinking, she enjoyed the feeling, letting go of every tension in her body, feeling each muscle relax. The comfort she was overwhelmed with was addictive. She started experiencing numbness at the extremity of her fingers and toes but still, she wouldn't pull out from the general relaxing sensation. When she started feeling her fingers again they were surrounded by what felt like dirt. She tried to move her toes but felt a resistance.

She soon had trouble breathing, when she opened her eyes she couldn't open her lids and she shortly understood she was covered, or more precisely, buried in the dirt. It was humid and heavy soil. She started suffocating and tried to pull out. She tried to move her arms around as if to unbury herself from where she was. She was frantically gesticulating to break free when she felt something warm around her hand and a weight lift her from behind her neck. She felt she was being lifted. Before the light penetrated through her lids she heard the faint whispered voice she had known too well, it said:

"Save me."

Then she made out another familiar voice breaking through the auditive haze repeating her name over and over again. She knew it was Samuel, she felt his warmth but she didn't want to open her eyes. Being in his arms made her feel safe and she didn't want him to let her go. So she lay there for a while. His hand kept touching her forehead to check if she was breaking up with a fever. His fingers accidentally stroke her cheek and she felt a warm vibration run through her entire body. She lifted her hand to trap his on her cheek. He did not resist. He pulled her closer and she fell asleep in his arms.

Samuel watched her sleep peacefully worried and knowing she would not be liberated from Koko's spirit, no matter how many miles away. Koko had chosen Estelle and would not let go until she was done. He had to stand by her through all this. She could not realize how much she needed his help. His being there for her to be pulled out of the abysses of the apparitions was vital. He did not know how or when all this would end. But he did know it would have to be in Blackmont and not Seattle. Her being far from the cradle of Koko's death would make the process longer and more painful. Koko had been dead for years and was now filled with anger and revenge. She was desperate to pass to her final rest, tired of wandering like a stray soul longing for salvation. Her fury could become dangerous if Estelle continued to lock her out.

Estelle awoke in her bed with a terrible headache. She soon noticed Samuel was asleep next to her. She studied the lines on his face, his fierce features betrayed him. She did not know many men who were that protective without ulterior motive. His silence and straight-talking could be defying but she didn't mind. She pulled closer to him and pulled his arm around her and gave into slumber.

Samuel opened one eye but pretended he was still sleeping. He didn't think it would be reasonable given the circumstances to slip into something even more complicated than it already was. He liked Estelle very much, what man wouldn't. But he also knew Taylor had opened his heart to her and that was the ultimate reason he would never even think of anything more. He was there to help her as he felt concerned and obligated to do so. He, after all, had called upon his sister to reveal the truth.

Estelle was pulled out of her sleep by her phone ringing. It was Dan. She wondered what time it was. It was noon. She felt drowsy. Samuel was gone. She didn't answer Dan's call, she would call him back when she'd had coffee. She got out of bed and took a quick warm shower. Samuel was in the kitchen and serving lunch when she entered the kitchen.

"You're up, I was just about to wake you up," he said in his distant way.

She smiled at him not surprised by his abruptness anymore.

"Thanks, I am starving," she said as she sat down at the

table and told him to join her. They ate in silence and when she was just about to take her last bite he broke out and said:

"You know you have to come back to Blackmont sooner or later if you want it or not."

"I thought we already had this conversation," she shot back annoyed by his pushiness. "I've already spent way too much time out there chasing ghosts. I really need to get on with my life. I'm alive, she's not." Estelle's dry tone and harsh words resonated in her ears.

"I'm sorry," she added grabbing his hand, "I didn't mean it that way, really, it's just that I don't see the point. I get that it's important for your mourning, but she's been gone for years, you've got to let go."

"You really don't understand, do you," he said calmly. "She's the one who's not going to let go of you no matter how hard you ignore it and how far you run.

"You're crazy, I'm done with this. I've got tons of work to do so please stop it and leave."

She took her phone and went up to her bedroom. She needed to return Dan's call but first, she had to calm down. It took ages for her to decide and make that call.

"Hey, you called," she said in a sweet voice when he answered.

"Yeah, just wanted to see how you were doing."

"I'm good, started working on some new material. Getting it together but I'm still tired from the accident and my attention span is still a bit dodgy."

"Yeah, I guess that's normal, it wasn't a small accident. As a matter of fact, you should maybe go see someone to help you. Maybe a check-up to make sure everything's ok. Not to worry you but sometimes little aches or traumas can cause damage in the long run if you don't attend to them."

"I guess you're right, I probably should do that and get it out of the way."

"Let me know if you need anything even if it's just company. I'm here don't hesitate."

"Thanks, Dan, will do."

"Take care, I'll call you tomorrow."

"Ok, you too."

His voice and words were soothing compared to what had just blown between Samuel and her. She wondered if Samuel took her words seriously and if he had already left. She tried to listen carefully to hear if there was any sort of noise coming from downstairs but none she could make out. She waited another few minutes and decided to check. Samuel was sitting stoically in the living room. He didn't look in her direction even though he knew she was there. He let her walk towards him and then looked up into her eyes.

"I know this is a lot for you to deal with, believe me, I am here to help you. The sooner this all ends the sooner you will be free to get on with your life but for now, you aren't free. You just think you are."

Estelle did not reply. She just stood there letting his words ring and repeat themselves, trying to make sense of it all.

"But why me, why do I have to cope with this. I didn't ask for anything," she broke down and cried.

"You did Estelle, you did ask for something. Spirits don't enter un-welcomed or uncalled upon."

She looked at him blankly.

"What do you mean?" she said, tears running down her red swollen cheeks.

He held her hands and explained:

"Well, my guess is, when you lost control of your car that night you called for help, I believe you died but came back. You got your life back in exchange for helping Koko pursue her revenge so that she could finally rest in peace. Your life does not belong to you until that is achieved."

Estelle ran the scene over in her head, trying to make out the forgotten pieces of what had exactly happened that night. She was tired and lost and the weather was getting worse. She was looking for a place to stop until the storm went by but nothing showed up except that apparition. She avoided the silhouette unsure of what it was and lost control of the vehicle, for a split second before hitting the tree she thought she was going to die, crashing in the ravine and she prayed. She then hit the tree and blacked out.

"Maybe I did call for help but the accident was caused by something. I was avoiding something. I thought someone was on the road."

"Koko probably provoked it so you could help her but you also called for her when you prayed."

"So what am I supposed to do? Do I have to go back there? What if it takes months, I can't do that."

"You're going to have to find a way," he answered.

Estelle returned to her room to think and rest. Each word and vision dancing in front of her. How was she going to deal with this? Dan would never forgive her for going back, not now that Spencer gave it a go for the record. She had to be writing and recording. There's no way she could pull something off without having to tell a huge lie. She couldn't possibly speak of this to anyone or she'd probably find herself interned and under sedatives. They'd say it's a post-traumatic shock, that she needs to be medicated and watched over.

| 33 |

When Estelle woke again that afternoon she still hadn't come up with a solution. She took another quick shower to wash off all the questions and doubts. Then she felt refreshed and inspired. She went into her home-studio and grabbed her guitar. She realized she hadn't held it in a while and that it almost felt strange. She played along with it, just strumming and trying to find chords that inspired her. She started to loop three chords and sang random words and after a few attempts, she had a melody set in. She pressed record and repeated endlessly trying, adding, and playing around with it. The song came easily. She was surprised. The song was melancholic. She sang it over and over again and finally recorded to cut a quick demo on her Protools. She left the vocals dry as Dan hated it when she added too many effects on her demos. As she waited for the bounce to finish she quickly noted the lyrics:

On a lonely road in the middle of nowhere
I found myself when I got lost
I found you, you, my mysterious host
Stranded in this icy air

Discovering the warmth under the frost
Where does it end
And where does it begin?
I can no longer pretend
So I stand here begging you to

Let me in
Let me into you
Let me in
Let me inside you

You let me in and gave meaning to my life
I let you in the cracks of my heart
Fearing the day we would be torn apart
Like the strike of a knife

I felt there was something right from the start
Why did it end
And why did it begin?
I could no longer pretend
And I should've stood there begging you to

Keep me in
Keep me into you
Keep me in
Keep me inside you

She sent both the lyrics and demo by email to Dan. She then waited anxiously to hear back from him. The seconds and minutes turned into half an hour and still no news from Dan. She was afraid he would not like it. Maybe she wasn't objective anymore, maybe she sent it out too quickly and should have waited to listen to it again tomorrow with fresh ears. All her doubts rose again. Dan called, she waited for a few rings before she answered.

"Hey," she said.

"I got your song. It's nice, really nice. I've got some ideas for it already if you could just send me the stems or just the dry vocal I will try something out."

"Sure glad you like it," she said relieved. "I'll send that out now."

"Keep it up, if you send me a song like this one every day we're going to have a hell of a record."

"I'll do my best," she answered freshly regaining confidence.

She bounced the dry vocal and sent it to him as he had requested. She then felt emptied and decided to stop for the day. It was already quite late. She went downstairs, feeling satisfied but still worried about what she would have to be doing. She couldn't make up her mind. Samuel was sweet and she was glad he was around. He had made dinner and was waiting for her to come down. They ate together simply avoiding the subject. Estelle played around with her cold pasta. Samuel watched her but said nothing, as usual. She snapped out of her thoughts when an idea hit her. She turned it over in her head to make sure it was possible and decided to give it a shot. It must have read on her face as Samuel was looking at her waiting for her to explain.

"I think I have an idea," she said.

She briefly explained it to Samuel who seemed to think it was a good idea as well. She now had to see if she could get away with it. To do so she had to ask Dan. She had to find the best way to ask him so that it sounded like a good idea. She gave herself until the next day to get her arguments together and talk to him. There was a good chance he would accept. She just had to find the right words.

| **34** |

Taylor had never been so spiritual in his thoughts. He was now asking himself metaphysical questions he had never thought he would. He always looked upon these things with distant amusement and nonsense. And yet, there he was, at that very point of his life, in presence of all these signs and unanswered questions. It was as if a whole new world was blossoming before him. A vast world of possibilities. His entire life he had learned and tried hard to keep away from his interests as he knew he was the obsessive kind. Therefore, he kept it all at a distance so that nothing would penetrate and trigger his obsession.

He felt he was in danger. He was afraid to lose control over himself eating all his energy in his hunt for the Truth. All the questions he had let slip and slide over the years. All the signs he had ignored and shut out to avoid facing the questions. And all the disregard had led him to that point.

Alone in the middle of nowhere. No one by his side to help him, to guide him, to love him, and he had no one to love. The loneliness he had looked upon as a friend was now becoming an enemy. A ball and chain that kept him imprisoned.

A heavy knock on the door startled him. He had been absorbed, he felt his brain was going to explode. He rubbed his face and slapped his cheeks as he walked to open the door.

"Allister?" he said shamefully, feeling sorry he hadn't called up to excuse himself for his absence.

"Boy, I just came out to check up on you, see if everything's alright."

"Yeah, I'm so sorry, I meant to call and time just flew by and I was busy and tired."

"There's no worries, son, just needed to see for myself how you were putting up. I told you to take all the time you needed, so you just do that," he said tapping Taylor's shoulder.

"I see you got a new computer there," he said as he sat in the armchair closest to the fireplace.

"Yeah, I went to Missoula for a few errands and since the old one wasn't working that well, I got this one. It's simple and fast."

"Good, I didn't realize you had any use for a computer outside of work, I sure wouldn't know what to do with it except type a report," Tim said smiling.

Allister stayed a while asking questions about the girl and Samuel and if he had any news from them. Taylor replied both by the negative and it kept his spirit rather low thinking of it and talking about it. Allister felt his pain and contained emotions so he stopped talking about it and switched to more conversational subjects.

Allister's visit did keep his mind off his new obsession and it did do him good to be talking to someone real. He realized how much he missed company. He missed Estelle. He wondered if she thought of him and if she missed him at all.

He looked through her little notebook again wishing he could call her. Allister must've had Dan's number and through Dan, he could get hers. But he couldn't get himself to do it. What would he say to her? He was afraid the telephone would break the magic. He didn't want to hear her voice over the phone, it would only emphasize the distance between them. He wanted to see her, feel her and touch her. Feel her presence and energy flow through him like it had when she was there. He played the scene in his head of going to Seattle to meet her there, to surprise her. He played each possible scenario over and over again. In one she would jump into his arms and cry, in the other, she would just stand there surprised and distant. That was the one he feared.

He noticed he had completely sunk into his thoughts, forgetting about Allister, not having listened to a word he had said. He felt ashamed when Allister's silence and insistent stare pulled him out of his reveries. He excused himself blaming the lack of sleep lately. He could read the worry in Allister's eyes. He did not know what to add. There was nothing more to say. Allister finally dismissed himself insisting on the fact that Taylor was always welcome whenever he needed. Taylor accompanied him to the front door, the lack of sleep making him slow and hazy. He watched him drive away and stood there gazing outside, feeling guilty not having taken care of Shakespeare but he did not have the energy. He could hardly walk back to his room without pausing.

| 35 |

"He's changed, something about him is different, I can't explain," the voice said over the phone.

"What do you mean? Do you think he knows something?"

"I'm not sure, I don't think so but I have a bad feeling about it."

"You're worrying me; I've never felt you worried about anything. Not even after the accident."

"I know, but maybe the old age and the guilt is coming to the surface. I may be imagining things. But I have got a gut feeling something's going to happen."

"I really don't see how anything could come out, not after all these years, and no evidence or trace of anything. You should take a break and relax."

"Maybe you're right but I know my gut feelings, they're usually always true."

"We'll be dead and buried before anything is discovered, believe me."

"That Indian boy sure knows how to stir me up, I tell you. He comes and goes without a trace."

"His no danger."

"Not for the moment, but I'd keep an eye on him."

"Have you checked that the papers are still there?"

"Every day since the accident, they are still there, untouched."

"Then what are you worried about?"

"We should destroy them."

"No, we can't do that!"

"It's the only evidence."

"I know, but we can't do that."

| **36** |

The forest was blooming, covered with fresh dew and golden vapor from the morning sun. The air was cool and damp and each footstep was slightly sinking into the soil with a light squishy sound. She walked slowly and tried to find where the sound of running water was coming from. She kept searching and finally got to a river. A worn-out sign indicated "welcome to Flathead River, no littering."

The water was vigorous, she watched the water flowing past her in a half-hypnotic state. In the water, the quick flow slowly turned into a slow movement and became placid. She watched as something seemed to be forming in front of her in the water. A flow of water started rising like a geyser and formed a silhouette. Estelle stepped back when she heard the familiar voice. There she was, Koko, all made of water, a perfect replica. The scene was magical.

"Don't be afraid," said the ghostly voice.

Estelle watched and waited.

"You must bring Taylor here. You must tell him it is hidden here."

"But what is hidden?" Estelle asked confused.

"The proof."

"The proof of what? What should we be looking for and where?"

"Bring Taylor here and he will find it."

Those were her last words as the silhouette of water fell back into the river and the ringing of an alarm brought her back to her bedroom. She had been dreaming.

She couldn't make it out. She had to tell Samuel so she jumped out of bed and ran down to the living-room where Samuel was sound asleep. She almost jumped on him and scared him to death. He gasped and took a few minutes to adapt and make out what was happening.

"I had a dream!" she yelled.

"Ok, calm down," he said as he lifted her from his chest so he could breathe properly.

He sat up, rubbed his eyes, and tried to wake as best he could so he could concentrate on what she was about to tell him.

"Ok, I'm ready, go ahead," he said looking at her.

"It was Koko, well not exactly, she was made of water, I was walking somewhere, near a river, Flatbed or something."

"Flathead River?"

"Yes, exactly!" she yelled.

"Could you just speak softer," he said cringing.

"Oh sorry, you know the place?" she asked in an extremely soft voice.

"Of course, we'd always hang out there with Taylor and Koko."

"Well, she said I had to bring Taylor there because that's where the evidence was and that he would find it."

Samuel stared at her as the words she just said echoed in his waking brain.

Estelle looked at him impatiently, waiting for a reaction, an explanation but nothing came. He froze deep in thought. She knew better than to interrupt him in those moments so she just sat there waiting for him to come back to her.

It felt very long and Estelle grew weary. She stood and paced back and forth till she was tired of waiting again. So as a habit she went to make coffee for both of them. She lit a cigarette as the coffee was dripping and Samuel still thinking.

The noise of the ticking hands of the kitchen clock took up all the space with the boiling water dripping into the pot. Each drop of coffee doubled by the click of the clock. It was driving Estelle crazy expecting Samuel to start explaining at any moment but the moment never came. He sat there and she stared at him from the kitchen. When it was ready she served two cups of hot steaming coffee and sat next to Samuel. She put her hand on his shoulder and pinched it. He kept his head down to avoid looking at her.

Finally, she heard the sound of his voice, it was low and shaky.

"I don't know what to make of it," he said.

"I guess we have to go see for ourselves and bring Taylor," she answered as she pulled him close to her to comfort him.

She hadn't seen Samuel so fragile before. The situation felt awkward but she was relieved there was another side to him than the fierceness he hid behind all the time. He was young when he lost his sister and she imagined how tough it must have been on him. She now had found the courage to call Dan up. She had to take Samuel and Taylor there and get it over with. It all seemed so unreal when she gave it more thought. But then she enjoyed the strangeness of it all. She felt special, why would someone or something choose her as a medium. She, who didn't believe in anything. She, who never read one word of a spiritual book, be it religion or esoteric. Had it not been for Samuel's insisting and persuasion she would have continued to ignore it all and think they were just anodyne dreams. Nothing more.

| **37** |

Estelle took a warm shower and got ready, she hadn't felt such a rush in a while. She was not going to call Dan but instead, she was going to go to his house so they could talk face to face. She blackened her eyes and put red lipstick on. She grabbed her purse and leather jacket and ran down the stairs. Samuel lifted his head and let escape a "wow". She smiled and said she'd be back later.

She had run out the door before he could say anything else. She went down to the garage and sat behind the wheel. She hadn't even had the chance to drive her new rental since she had brought it home. Now that she was inside she hesitated to turn the engine on. As she started the engine flashes of the accident came to her. At first, she thought it was her accident but she couldn't recognize anything. It wasn't her car, it wasn't the same road, there were two elder people in the car with her.

They were all happy and all of a sudden a blast, a huge

deafening sound echoed and everything started shaking. She lost control of the vehicle and it flipped to the side as flames crawled over the windows and the temperature increased until the burning feeling reached her. Through the smoke, she saw two men watching and walking towards the car. She made signs and cried for help until one huge explosion brought her back to her garage.

She sat there analyzing what she had just seen. She calmed herself down by breathing slowly. She opened the garage door and pulled out. The drive to Dan's was easy and quick, she had driven there so many times since she moved to Seattle. She knows that drive better than going to the nearest supermarket. When she arrived at the entrance of his residence the guard recognized her and started a kind conversation. She pulled up into his driveway and parked next to his car. She breathed slowly again before getting out of the car and ringing his doorbell.

"What a nice surprise!" Dan exclaimed as he opened the door and lay his eyes on a bright and beautiful Estelle. The Estelle he had met a while ago. The Estelle he hadn't seen in a long time. He let her in and gave her a friendly hug. She held him tighter than he expected and it arose him. He kept calm and countenanced. She walked in as she was very familiar with the place. Dan's place was very modern, slightly cold but in a different way than hers. There wasn't a lot of furniture and everything was white and grey. She sat on the armchair she would always sit on. He systematically made both of them an expresso and sat in front of her.

"So, what brings me the joy of your visit?"

She sipped the expresso slowly and prepared herself.

"I need to talk to you about something important," she said as her hands played with the tiny grey cup.

"I'm all ears," he answered slightly worried.

"Well, I was thinking of what you and Spencer said." She paused and looked at him as he nodded for her to continue. "I'm persuaded that it would do me good to go out someplace different to write new songs. Like in the countryside. Wake up and only have that to do, no other obligations or distractions. I need to resource. I would send you all the tracks I write and we could work like that."

Dan said nothing and thought about it.

"Hmmm. I don't know if it's a good idea that you go out somewhere all alone, especially after what you've been through. Now, I completely understand the point and I think it's a great idea. I just don't think you should be alone for the time being. And that is the only thing worrying me." he answered honestly.

"Please Dan, please, I've thought this through and I really need to do this. I really need to get away and think about my music, get new material. I'll be fine and we'll Skype every day," she pleaded.

Dan couldn't resist Estelle and he knew she knew it. He did want to please her but he was worried.

"Trust me, please," she whispered.

Dan sighed and said: "Alright, but you better not forget to call and give me news every single day."

"Promise Dan," she said as she jumped into his arms and squeezed as hard as she could.

Dan didn't know if he should hug her back, still afraid of the misinterpretation. So he gently wrapped his arms around her and left her in control. Estelle was deeply excited but afraid of this new turn. What would she find up there near the river? And how would seeing Taylor again feel like? All the questions and all the panic popped out right there while still with Dan. Dan didn't notice anything. He was having trouble resisting the close encounter with the woman he was attracted to but couldn't have. When she finally let go and sat back none of them knew what to say. The silence began to feel uncomfortable so Estelle jumped up to her feet and said in a voice full of thrill:

"I better get to it then!"

"The floor is yours hun," he said with the most excited tone he could fake to hide his worry.

She gave him another quick hug before leaving as swiftly as she had come.

On her way back she stopped by the mall to get warm clothes and a pair of good boots. When she came back home Samuel was ready and waiting. She told him briefly how things went as she finished packing up her things. They went into the car and Estelle started driving. A few minutes passed until she remembered the vision she had had on the way to Dan's that morning. The car crash and the fire and the men in the distance. She tried to tell Samuel the entire vision without skipping any details. As she was telling it she could feel Samuel becoming tense but she knew she had to let him know of everything she saw as he was the only one who could interpret her visions and give meaning to them.

They were a team, they had to work together. She knew they had a special relationship. Samuel was fixing the road, his eyes darker and fiercer than usual. His lips were stiff and his jaw was tense. If you looked close enough you could even see the vein on his temple popping. His fists were clenched, nothing about him was relaxed. Estelle was just waiting for him to explode. His anger filled the car. She preferred to stay silent as he worked himself out of it. She knew there was nothing she could do, he was all fire. A few miles later she could feel he had slightly cooled off. She squeezed his hand and he relaxed. No words were needed. Samuel would speak when he'd have something to say. There was no forcing anything out of him before that. So Estelle concentrated on the road and sang to the songs that were playing on the radio. After a few hours' drive, Samuel took the wheel so Estelle could rest. Estelle fell asleep lulled by the smooth drive and the music. Samuel did not talk throughout the drive.

As they entered Montana the weather got colder. They stopped to eat. Still, Samuel did not talk. Estelle was now used to it and it didn't bother her. She liked to watch him, his expressions were always deep and his moves strong and economized. He was swift but gentle. She liked everything about him. He was very intense and dramatic to observe. She wondered if it was part of his native American heritage. Estelle finished her salad and ate some bread and butter before ordering a cup of coffee to go. Samuel was still finishing his meal. It was already night when they started driving again. As they approached the place Estelle had crashed she clutched the seat and held tight. Samuel was calm and kept an eye on her silently. Her heart was pounding fast. She didn't know if it was the drive past the accident or if it was because she was going to see Taylor again.

As Samuel pulled up into the driveway and they saw Taylor's car parked there they exchanged a glance. Samuel told Estelle to go inside and that he'd take care of the luggage. He felt her panic but did not suggest help. She knew there was no insisting after that point so she grabbed her purse and walked to the door. Her finger stopped right in front of the doorbell. And the door opened before she had the time to press it. They both stood there staring at each other blankly. Taylor was slightly in shock at the sight of Estelle. He rubbed his eyes to make sure he wasn't dreaming. She was still there in front of him. He didn't know what to say. Estelle just stood there too and when Samuel walked up to the door and saw them like that he said:

"Well, did the cat catch your tongues or what?" As he pushed through with the luggage.

Taylor put his arm over Estelle's shoulder and led her in. As she stepped in the warm fire caressed her face and she instantly felt home. Samuel put the luggage down behind the couch and walked up to Taylor, they gave each other a manly hug. They all sat down next to the fire as Samuel and Estelle explained everything to him. Taylor listened to them carefully. Deep down, he felt happy to have both of them back with him. The house felt revived and warm. The house had come back to life just like Taylor, Estelle and Samuel had.

| **38** |

Estelle's eyes were fixed on the fire after her third glass of whisky. Taylor and Samuel were still deep in discussion, reminiscing the accident Koko and his parents had been in. Estelle listened to them vaguely and stared at each of them in turn. Her head was hazy with alcohol. Samuel gave a sign to Taylor to bring Estelle something to eat. Taylor instantly understood and brought snacks to the table. They all nibbled. Estelle fell asleep on Taylor's shoulder.

"So, you truly believe this is all real, that Koko is genuinely communicating with Estelle?" Taylor asked seriously.

"We wouldn't be here if we didn't think it was so. We have to see where she is leading us. Koko said that you would know where to look. What we are looking for, I don't know," Samuel answered.

"It's what we will find that I am worried about," he answered perplexed.

"We have to be open to see what she wants us to see. If we don't believe, it can't work," Samuel continued.

"I just don't know what she could possibly be trying to tell us."

"I'm sure she will give us the answer, she will tell us what happened that day. I've been trying to find out."

"Why should there be something to find out, it was an accident, Allister was clear and there was no doubt about it."

"We'll just wait and see what we will discover, and you have to embrace the truth that comes out no matter how difficult it might end up being."

"Tomorrow's going to be a big day so let's get some sleep," Samuel added as he headed to the bedroom.

Taylor carried Estelle to his bedroom and lay her on the bed. He took her jeans off, it reminded him of when he had first brought her home. He looked at her sound asleep. Her ruby hair on the white pillowcase. A flashback of the night of her accident. The streaks of her tattoo underneath her red shirt. He guessed her eyes and was surprised when she opened them briefly and turned around.

He hesitated for a while and went to bed next to her. He lay softly down on the other side of the bed so he didn't touch her. He kept still so he wouldn't wake her. His muscles tightened and wanted to move but he restrained himself from moving as long as his body would let him.

He finally relaxed and gave in to sleep. The night was calm except for the crackling of the wood-burning in the fire. The wind outside whistled on the window panes. The frost and snow were almost completely thawed. No spirit came to the house that night to interrupt the reunion. All slept in peace.

| 39 |

Samuel's sleep had been heavier than usual as if he were on the verge of finding peace. The answers he had so longed for and searched the world for were about to unfold. He had the gut feeling something was going to come into place. He had always felt Koko was going to come back to reveal the truth. Koko had been working on Blackfeet cultural preservation for as long as he could remember. She had boosted the young generation to embrace their Native American heritage with all it meant. She had been researching documents and stories to put together a history book for the school reservation so children were taught their history and the history of the land they were living on.

Everyone in the reservation loved Koko and how she brought back a certain pride to their lives. Of course, this also led to a number of enemies, who looked at her energy and curiosity as a potential threat. A feared uprising and revival of the tribe. No one would speak of it openly but behind closed doors, families, and friends would talk of Koko and her actions and researches. Samuel had always felt the look of the people in town when he or his sister were there. Taylor never noticed anything as he was too deep in his thoughts and dreams.

Taylor had always been a dreamer. There was nothing mean nor bad about him. Taylor had adopted Samuel instantly and he had always been comfortable in the reservation before the accident. He never stepped foot back there after the accident as the pain he wanted to shut out would have poured out if he had seen Koko's family. Samuel had taken his reaction as treason at the time. Now that he was old enough to understand the works of grief he did not hold a grudge against him. The only thing he did not understand was why he had done nothing to keep her memory alive.

He had trouble believing Taylor could shut out his entire life as he had done. The elders at the reservation explained to Samuel how mourning comes differently to people and that no one could be held responsible for that, as suffering is buried deep inside no matter what. Koko had practically raised Samuel. She was more than just a sister. She took him with her everywhere she went. He lived with her and Taylor. He had always been very mature. He had grown up with adults and became one very early on. He never spoke much but listened a lot.

His sister meant everything to him. When she died he wanted revenge so badly that the anger followed his every step. The only way to relieve it was to go far away. The time he spent in Africa had been a turning point in his mourning. He had found peace there after all he had been through. His work there had kept him busy and gave meaning to his life. Helping others kept his anger away and his mind off his quench for revenge. Coming back to Blackmont was like coming back into the past, heavy with sadness but also with the happiness of returning to his roots and to the people he loved. All but one, but his sister had come to him in a way and he could feel her there. He only hoped for one thing, that she also found peace and that Estelle would come out of this alive.

Many stories have told the dark truth of the dead coming to avenge themselves. Many had said that when a dead person comes to your dreams and leads you to them they will lead you to your own death. Samuel knew well of the dangers they were facing. He knew someone would be sacrificed, he just wanted that it be the traitors that would pay and not an innocent soul.

He trusted Koko but years of roaming between both worlds could darken the brightest of souls. Samuel will be there every step of the way to guide both Estelle and Taylor. They were both young souls and inexperienced with the world of spirits. Estelle, in particular, was very fragile and if things went wrong she would be in great danger. Taylor was such a detached soul that the harm would not be of much consequence. His main task was to watch over Estelle but he was confident as she had opened up to him and let him in.

She trusted him and he would be able to lead her through the darkness if needed. Koko had lost most of her strength and was now holding on to the little that was left for the finale. She would certainly appear to Estelle once at Flathead river and certainly for the last time.

It was Estelle's last vision that was misleading. In the car that took fire, the two men she saw in the distance. He did have an idea, what he had thought deep down inside was starting to become real. The reality was still something that would hit him even if it had lingered in his mind. The different scenarios he had imagined but the evidence and the reasons why would never fit. What would the motive be? No matter how much he despised and suspected the people in town he could not imagine what would be that important to lead to the silencing of Koko and Taylor's parents. Why Taylor's parents? That was the main mystery. If Koko had been alone in the car, he would have been certain that it had been intentional.

He was impatient to find the answers, to finally know what really happened that day. The fact that no one looked for the causes of the accident had made his doubts grow at the time. Case closed, loss of control over the vehicle. Koko was used to driving those parts and the spot of the accident was not a dangerous place. No turn, no hill, no obstacles anywhere. There was no sign of anything on the road or around the road that could have caused a car to turn over and explode, at least that was what they stated in the official record, and since no one asked for further information the record was closed and filed almost instantly. No one ever mentioned anything about it again and everyone avoided the subject discreetly. And time erased any shadow of a doubt, any black spot.

| **40** |

As the sun rose through the windows it tickled Taylor's eyelids, he felt a weight on his chest. As he looked down he saw shiny red hair all over his arm. Estelle's head was niched between his chest and his arm. He slowly bent his arm to move some of the hair from her eyes. She looked peaceful and happy. She released a gentle sigh and stretched her lips into a tiny and brief yawn. Her eyelids trembled a little before she tried to open them. When she did the sun burned them as she tried to look up to Taylor. Their eyes met and Taylor stroke her hair back gently, before he had time to think, she approached her lips to his and kissed him softly. Electricity ran down his spine and he pulled her head closer to his, holding her head in the palm of his hand.

They lay in a tight embrace for a while until Samuel interrupted them by bulging in all ready to go. His eagerness to get things over with filled the room and contaminated them. He did not need to say anything, he just left the room as abruptly as he had entered it and both Taylor and Estelle got out of bed to get ready.

When they came into the kitchen, breakfast was already served. No one spoke. Samuel was deep in thought and Estelle was nervous. Taylor, as usual, did not express much. They all feared the journey they were about to take into the world of the unknown and mysterious. Estelle had never been into dark arts and spiritism. She feared to believe, and she preferred not to see so she did not have to believe, but this time she had no choice. Deep down she hoped nothing would happen and that Samuel was wrong and that it was all just her imagination and his will to bury the past once and for all. She did understand Samuel but she wanted to avoid having to believe in things she did not want to believe in. She reluctantly chewed her last piece of toast as she was starting to feel a bit nauseous. She also felt slight dizziness and numbness in her limbs. She tried to fix her eyes on something to stop the spinning, she felt as if she were sea-sick.

The room and everything around her started rocking from side to side as if she were on a boat. She tried to concentrate and breathe deeply to fight nausea. She clutched her seat trying to make the spinning feeling go away. She felt the pressure pumping inside her forehead, giving her the impression her head was going to explode. She focused on deep conscious breathing. Both Samuel and Taylor noticed something was wrong with her. They tried talking to her, asking her if she was alright. But the voices were not audible. Her ears were whistling. She couldn't make out their words and her eyes too weak to make out any lip-reading. The headache and nausea were intensifying.

She could no longer fight it. She pushed them away and she ran to the sink where she was sick. She fell to the floor feeling empty and weak. Samuel ran to her and bent down soon after with a wet towel and dabbed her face and forehead. Taylor held a glass of water to her lips and forced her to drink. When she recuperated they both helped her get back up and sat her on the chair. She was feeling better. Samuel knew it was just the beginning but he said nothing. He acted calm as he always did. Half an hour passed before he got up silently and walked out. Taylor handed his hand out to Estelle to help her get up and follow him. All was done very solemnly.

Estelle was dressed in black jeans with a black and red silk corsage. Her lips were red and her eyeshadow was jet black making her eyes look emerald-green. She doubled the dose of perfume to cover the foul smell she still had in her nose. She slipped into her high black Doc Martens. They were worn out and faded but classy with the overall attitude she had. She got in the back of the car letting Samuel take the front seat next to Taylor.

Estelle noticed Samuel was wearing a ring she had never seen him wearing before. It was particularly colorful, ruby red, emerald green, sapphire blue, and amber yellow. When she asked him what it was he explained it was iniskim, or more popularly called ammolite. The Blackfeet tribe called it "buffalo stone" and had long believed it to possess amuletic powers. He added that it was commonly used in medicine bundles during ceremonies for its healing powers. He explained how some believed it detoxified the body by improving its flow of energy.

She examined it carefully, it was quite a big stone mounted on a thick silver ring. It had a non-geometrical form, it did not seem as if it had been cut into that shape. It was well polished as it was smooth and shiny. Her eyes were fixated on that stone during the entire drive. She was hypnotized by its colors.

As they pulled up she felt oppressed. She felt a heavy weight in her chest as if someone were squeezing her very tightly. Samuel opened the back door and held his hand out so she could jump out of the car. She reached to grab his hand with difficulty. When he held her the pain and weight lifted. She jumped to the ground liberated but as soon as he let go of her hand the weight and pain came back even harder. She limped behind like an old lady. She had been so absorbed by Samuel's ring during the drive that she had not noticed how dark and grey the sky had become. It felt like night. The wind was cold and it penetrated her weak pores not making it any easier for her to walk.

As they approached the river the wind grew stronger and the sky darker. Heavy drops of rain started falling. Each drop crashed hard on her face and felt like a rock. The pain grew sharper, she had more and more difficulty moving. She felt out of breath. She could not walk any further. When Taylor noticed she was lagging behind he ran back to her but the wind kept him away. He could not approach her. Gusts of wind blew him to the opposite side towards the river. Samuel did not seem affected by anything. He was able to reach Estelle and the moment he grabbed her, her strength came back, and she could walk with him.

A loud rumble filled the air, the thunderclap forced them

to cover their ears, all but Samuel, who remained unaffected by the elements. The flashing lightning followed almost instantly, striking the ground before them. Taylor crashed to his knees and covered his head in shock. The storm continued violently, the calm river water turned to heavy waves as Samuel and Estelle reached the edge. Samuel yelled out to Estelle:

"Is this the place you dreamed of?"

Estelle looked at him through her hair flying all over her face from the wind and rain and acquiesced.

He then gave her a sign to follow him, he was still holding her hand as he kneeled to the ground and sat on his knees, she followed and mimicked his every move. He then bowed down to the ground, his forehead touching the wet leaves. Estelle did the same hesitantly. He seemed as though he was in trance. Taylor was further away still on his knees watching the scene through the heavy rain. He saw Estelle glance at him before doing what Samuel told her to.

The sky darkened even more and the wind blew over the river as a pale misty light formed. Taylor had trouble making out and understanding what was happening. A darker silhouette appeared in the middle of the well of light. He made out a tall womanlike figure with what seemed like long hair flowing in the wind. There was nothing human-like nor ghost-like. Something unexplainable. The energy flowed into them directly, nothing could be seen through the human eye.

The silhouette pulled Taylor closer, aligning him to Estelle and Samuel. She communicated with him telepathically. Her words and feelings both flowed into him like electricity. Samuel could feel Estelle's strength diminishing, he started incantations to protect her and keep her on their side. Koko was using Estelle's energy to communicate with Taylor. Estelle's grip became loose and her body lost tension. She collapsed face down and unconscious.

Samuel pulled her close to him and he drew a circle around them both as he raised his ring towards the pale light, mumbling words in his native dialect. A distant siren sounded from the road behind them, they could not turn around to look and the visibility around them was blurry as if they had been immersed underwater. Samuel continued his mumbled chant when a loud crashing sound echoed from behind them. Samuel continued in a trance when the ground beneath them shook from what seemed to be an explosion.

All of a sudden the light disappeared, the wind fell, the water calmed and the sky cleared out almost instantly. Estelle was still out but Taylor remained completely still, his eyes staring at the spot where the pale light and silhouette had been. His jaw was relaxed and his palms open towards the sky. Samuel read the awe on his face. Koko had spoken, Taylor now knew something, something dark. The lines on his face were grave and he looked older. Samuel knew Koko was now gone, completely gone.

| 41 |

Samuel cautiously let go of Estelle ran to check up on Taylor. Taylor was in shock, his eyes and lips immobile. He shook his hand in front of his eyes but still no sign of Taylor inside the body. He yelled into his ear and still nothing. In anger and pain, he started to shake Taylor's shoulders violently as if it would wake him from his sleep. Taylor's body did not respond. Samuel continued shaking, hitting, and crying. When Estelle opened one eye and saw Samuel brutally hitting Taylor she panicked. She crawled to them weakly, falling face down every yard. Her arms were too weak to carry her, she started yelling and begging Samuel to stop. He ignored her. He did not hear her, his grief was so intense. He could not lose Taylor. Not him, not the only person he had left. He crumbled to the ground crying. He was a wreck. When she finally reached them her heart was torn, torn by the expression on the mens' faces. She touched them and collapsed between them.

The energy and elements they had been confronted to were so strong that it had emptied them. Their bodies were sore and would not respond. Their souls were marked by the burst of information. When Taylor saw the light and felt the pulsing in his hand he slowly turned to see the scene around him. It was apocalyptical. There were leaves and dirt all over the place and Samuel and Estelle laying motionless beside him. As he turned the other way he made out a cloud of dark grey smoke and the heavy smell of gasoline filled his nostrils. He tried to decipher what the smoke was but the way his body and neck were positioned was too painful. He had to contortion himself and it hurt him. He tried to move but Samuel and Estelle's weight kept him down. His moving and gesticulations woke them.

When Samuel saw Taylor awake and moving he revived. His emotions were too strong to tame. He jumped to Taylor's throat and squeezed him so tightly Taylor had to unfasten his grip. When Samuel's euphoria faded away he too inhaled the gasoline. The smell was so strong they all started coughing. Samuel was the first on his feet; he then helped the other two up. Taylor helped Estelle lean on him as she was a lot weaker than them.

They all looked toward the smoke pinching their noses. As they approached the smell worsened making their eyes cry. The wind started clearing away some smoke and they started to decipher the scene before them. It was a car, completely burnt. A shiny object caught their eyes and Taylor bent down to pick it up. He dusted off the dirt and there it was, the sheriff's badge in the palm of his hand. At the very spot, Koko had pointed out to him. He now knew she had taken her revenge. She was now at peace. What she had told him he would never repeat. Not to Samuel, not to Estelle. Her words would remain within him forever. The peace she had found had also brought peace to him. He was now ready to live again. He threw the badge back onto the dirt where he had found it. In silence, he turned back to Estelle and Samuel, took Estelle by the hand and they slowly returned to the car. They all watched the burnt car slowly appear as the smoke cleared.

The drive back was silent. None of them spoke. Samuel drove without thinking, his eyes fixed on the road but his mind was lost in thought. Taylor was in the backseat holding Estelle, who had fallen asleep in his arms. His eyes were also fixed in an empty stare on the road. When they reach the cabin Taylor lay Estelle down gently on his bed. She was still very weak. Samuel soon followed with a small leather bag. He told Taylor to leave him alone with her. Taylor hesitantly left the room after kissing her burning forehead.

As he closed the door behind him he waited and listened but he heard no sound so he gave up and went out. Everything he had seen in his head was playing over and over again. All the things Koko had revealed to him were the darkest things he had ever had to deal with. Her pain and the truth he now knew made their way through him. Fate had not been the one to blame after all. The evils of mankind were always unexpected. The ones he trusted and loved were right by his side now and he would do everything in his power to keep them close and safe. It was never too late to find meaning in life, was it through pain or pleasure. He chose to clear the slate, start anew, leaving the past where it belonged. He would focus on the future. On Estelle and Samuel. On himself. It was time to let go and be true.

His eyes sparkled as he saw Samuel come out holding Estelle by the arm. She seemed different, they were all deeply changed but in a positive way. Apart from the strain and fatigue they were radiant and peaceful standing there in the orange sunset.

SPECIAL THANKS

I want to thank all those who have supported me and have taken the time to read, re-read, give feedback, and encourage me to write. A special thanks to the helpers! You know who you are. You helped me get this thing together and I am very thankful!